MYSTERY in the MUSEUM

by Virginia Frances Voight

When her widowed mother marries wealthy Oliver Payne, it is a great shock to sixteen-year-old Nancy Frost and she feels she can never be happy again. Her stepfather is kind and generous to her, but she finds him overbearing and domineering, although she becomes fond of his young daughter, Karen.

Nancy longs to be independent, so when a job in the local college's Museum of Natural History presents itself, she takes it gladly. Later, she learns that the museum is partially supported by her stepfather. At the museum she meets Dan Stevens, a brash young man who has a spoiled girl friend, and Alan Shelby, who reveals great hostility toward Mr. Payne. At a family dinner, Nancy discovers that there is a bitter and long-standing feud between her stepfather and his cousin Burton over the division of their grandmother's jewels. Burton feels that a valuable topaz necklace should have been his, but Oliver Payne has given it to Nancy's mother. During a reception at the museum the necklace disappears!

The story unfolds against the background of the museum with its huge Hall of Dinosaurs and fabulous mineral-collection room, and the mystery comes to a climax on a night of storm and terror. two have made great strides in meeting the challenges of the adult world.

MYSTERY IN THE MUSEUM

Virginia Frances Voight

MYSTERY in the MUSEUM

FUNK & WAGNALLS COMPANY, INC. | NEW YORK

Other books by the same author

UNCAS: *Sachem of the Wolf People*
TREASURE OF HEMLOCK MOUNTAIN
THE MISSING $10,000 BILL
MYSTERY AT DEER HILL

To my friend Dottie Susan Johnsen

Contents

MYSTERY IN THE MUSEUM

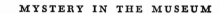

A new family

Standing at her window, lost in unhappy thoughts, Nancy Frost became aware that someone else had entered the bedroom. Immediately on the defensive, she swung around. The intruder was Karen, but she was paying no attention to Nancy at the moment; she had picked a cocky little stuffed tiger off the bed and was cuddling it under her chin. Anger and outrage flashed in Nancy's green eyes.

"Put that down this instant!"

She strode across the room, her fingers itching to snatch the tiger away and smack the younger girl's pink cheeks.

Karen looked up, startled by the angry sound of her stepsister's voice.

"I only wanted to pet him—he's so cute . . ."

Silently, her lips set in a tight line, Nancy held out her hand, and Karen hastily pushed the stuffed tiger at her. Nancy seized it and crushed it against her chest.

"After this, please stay out of my room!" she snapped.

She felt almost panicky. There had to be someplace where she could get away from these Paynes!

Karen looked as if she had been struck. She backed toward the door.

"I will—I will," she promised. "Truly, Nancy, I didn't mean to intrude."

Her eyes filled with tears. She was plump and pretty, with dimpled cheeks and a fluff of red-gold curls. Although she was almost fifteen, she seemed much younger than Nancy, who had just turned sixteen.

Karen stopped in her retreat to the door to give her new stepsister a bewildered look. Nancy felt a pang of guilt. She remembered how Karen had greeted her with a kiss when she had arrived from Vermont with her mother the night before, how she had said happily, "I'm so glad to have a sister."

But I'm not her sister!

No, and she wanted no part of Karen or any other Payne. She hated Oliver Payne, her new stepfather, and she was determined to hate his daughter and his house; she must live here from now on, but it could never be home. Oh, how could her mother have gone and married Oliver Payne, with his booming voice and bossy ways?

I can't stand it! Nancy thought in despair.

She flew at Karen, as she would have liked to fly at Karen's father, and pushed her out of the room, slamming the door shut quickly. Alone, she leaned against it, squeezing the little tiger, which her own father had given her long ago and which had been her mascot ever since. The tears she had held back so resolutely ever since she had entered this house now overflowed her eyes and slid down her cheeks to fall on the tiger's silky fur.

Nancy's father, a free-lance commercial artist, had worked for Mr. Payne's company, and sometimes when business brought him to New York, Mr. Payne had taken Mr. and Mrs. Frost out to dinner and the theater. In those happy days, he had been only a name to Nancy.

Then, when Charles Frost had been killed in an auto accident three years ago, Oliver Payne had called on his widow to offer condolences and advice on how to handle her affairs. Amy Frost, stunned by her sudden loss, had been grateful to the big, hearty man. Easy-going Charles Frost had made a good living, but he had been a free spender, too. After his affairs were put in order, there was little left to provide for his widow and daughter. Nancy and her mother moved out of their large apartment to a small one in another part of the city.

"We mustn't blame Daddy," Mrs. Frost said, as she talked over the necessary changes with Nancy. "He was careless with money, but he was very good to us, and he expected to be providing for us for many years to come." Nancy nodded. The lump that had swelled in her throat, made it difficult for her to speak. She wouldn't have cared about giving up anything, if only Daddy could have been with them again.

Amy Frost found a job in an office, but not a brilliant job. She was not at home in the business world, and her earnings were barely adequate to support Nancy and herself. Nancy helped by baby-sitting to provide her own spending money and some of her clothes. Because she was slow in making friends at her new school, she and her mother grew even closer together during those difficult days.

Whenever business brought Oliver Payne to New York, he called on Mrs. Frost and took her and Nancy out to dinner at some expensive restaurant. He was a ruddy, handsome man with a shock of iron-gray hair. Under his heavy brows, his eyes were friendly but sharp. He told the Frosts about his young daughter, Karen, and pulled out a gold-mounted alligator case, proud to show them snapshots of her and of their home in Glendale Falls. His wife had died when Karen was five, and his sister, Florence, who had made her home with them, had taken over the management of their household. Now, suddenly, Florence had announced that she was going to get married.

"Karen and I will feel quite lost in our big house without her," said Mr. Payne.

At Christmas, Mr. Payne sent a huge box of chocolates to Nancy and roses to Mrs. Frost. Nancy felt the first pang of jealousy as she watched her mother carefully lift the roses from their nest of ferns. Her cheeks flushed faintly and a tiny smile hovered on her lips. She looked young, almost girlish, at that moment.

How pretty Mother is, Nancy thought. No wonder Mr. Payne admires her!

Suddenly a stirring of alarm mingled with her jealousy. She felt as if she were being threatened with the loss of something infinitely precious to her, and she crossed the room to throw her arms around her mother.

The next time Mr. Payne called, Nancy refused to go out to dinner with her mother and him.

"Exams tomorrow—I've got to cram tonight," she explained shortly. After the sound of Mr. Payne's deep voice and her mother's low laughter had died away in the hall, Nancy burst into tears. She sensed that Mr. Payne was bringing a drastic change into her life and that there was not a thing she could do about it.

They returned at an early hour, but Nancy was already in bed and pretending to be asleep. She knew her mother would want to talk about the evening and she could not bear to hear her quoting Mr. Payne or saying how sorry she felt for him and Karen, alone in their big house.

In the weeks that followed, it did not help Nancy's low spirits to know that her mother was corresponding with Mr. Payne. The very sight of one of the thick white envelopes addressed to her mother in strong, dashing handwriting was enough to make Nancy's heart pound with a sickening thud. At first her mother was eager to read her parts of the letters, but Nancy refused to listen. She simply could not pretend to be interested in Mr. Payne or his droopy daughter, Karen.

It was May when the influenza epidemic struck, giving Nancy such a bad time that she missed the last month of school. Her mother asked for a spring vacation, so she could stay home and nurse her. Flowers, books, and fruit arrived from Mr. Payne, and he telephoned often to inquire about the patient and to talk to her mother. Nancy was too ill to let these things bother her. The only important thing in the world was that her mother was near.

Gradually Nancy's normally good health returned to her. When she was strong enough to go out, Aunt Kathy, her mother's sister, drove down from Vermont to take her back for two weeks in the country.

Nancy's mother hugged her hard when they said good-by. "I love you very much, darling," she whispered. "Now be careful and don't overdo."

Nancy was fond of her aunt and enjoyed visiting her, so the two weeks passed swiftly. Her mother was expected for an overnight visit and the two would then travel home together. An affectionate note had asked Nancy and Aunt Kathy not to meet her at the bus station in the village. She would be driving.

Nancy's high spirits took an immediate slide.

"That means that Mr. Payne will be driving her," she told Aunt Kathy unhappily. Her aunt looked troubled and started to say something. Then, instead, she put her arm around Nancy and pulled her close.

When Nancy's mother arrived, however, she was alone. Alone, but in a beautiful new car. She parked the car in Aunt Kathy's driveway and sprang out to meet Nancy, who came running from the house.

"Oh, darling, how well you look!" Mother cried joyfully.

"You look wonderful, too," said Nancy.

Her mother was wearing a smart new suit and hat. Her face, with its fine features and white-rose complexion, looked young and lovely.

"Where did you borrow that gorgeous car?" Nancy went on.

"Nancy . . ." Her mother held her hand tightly. "Nancy, the car was a wedding present."

"A wedding present?" But Nancy understood, even before her mother's next words.

"From my husband and your new father. Oliver Payne and I were married last week."

It was what Nancy dreaded most in the world to hear, and yet, in her heart, she knew she had been expecting just this news. She stared at her mother, her lips trembling.

"It means a wonderful life for us, dear." There was a pleading note in her mother's soft voice. "Perhaps I should have told you before, but you take things so hard, Nancy."

Nancy bit her lips to stop their silly quivering. She heard her mother's voice flowing on, telling about the beautiful home in Glendale Falls, telling about Oliver Payne's kindness and generosity.

Mother is happy, thought Nancy. She's had a hard time since Daddy died, but now she's happy again. She won't have to work at that job she hated so much. She can be a homemaker again. She won't have to plan and skimp to make the money stretch. She can have pretty clothes and a nice social life. It's the kind of life she's most suited for, and, Nancy Frost, you're a toad if you do anything to spoil her happiness!

Although she couldn't keep a few tears from slipping out from under her eyelids, she brushed them swiftly away and hugged her mother and kissed her warmly.

MYSTERY IN THE MUSEUM 10

"We're going to be such a happy family," her mother said with relief in her voice.

At the breakfast table the next morning, Nancy asked to stay on with Aunt Kathy until school opened in Glendale Falls.

"It will give you time to get acquainted with K-Karen without me in the way," she said, trying to sound lighthearted.

Her mother shook her head. "As if you could ever be in the way, my darling. No, I think it best that you go home with me, and so does Oliver."

Nancy bit her lip. If Oliver Payne wanted her in Glendale Falls, that seemed to cinch the matter as far as her mother was concerned.

So here she was, and she could not deny that she had received a hearty welcome from Mr. Payne and Karen. Even Minnie Bell, the housekeeper, appeared to be very glad to see her.

"It'll be good for Karen to have another young person in the house," Minnie had told Nancy as they shook hands.

Nancy's mother, Mr. Payne, Karen, and Minnie had trooped upstairs together to show Nancy her bedroom, all apparently motivated by a single heartfelt desire— to see her happily settled in her new quarters. Her room and Karen's occupied one wing of the big colonial house, and they shared a pink-tiled bathroom. Nancy's was a large room with snowy Priscilla curtains at the three windows. The furniture was early American cherry wood—just what she would have chosen for herself. There was a wing chair in rose and green chintz to match the coverlet on the four-poster bed. The bookshelves were already partly filled with her own books.

"Do you like it, dear?" her mother asked anxiously.

"Of course she likes it, Amy," Mr. Payne put in before Nancy could reply. "How could she help but like this room after all the thought and effort you put into getting it ready for her?"

Nancy's cheeks burned, but she said truthfully, "It's a beautiful room, Mother."

"Good, good," Mr. Payne replied for his wife. "We want you to be happy here, Nancy." He threw one arm about Nancy and the other about Karen and gave them a bearlike hug. "Our two girls," he said to his wife with intense satisfaction.

Nancy stood stiffly in the circle of her stepfather's arm and stepped away as soon as she could without offending him. She heaved a sigh of relief when at last they all went away and left her alone. She was even glad to see her mother go, for keeping up a front for her sake was more exhausting than a ten-mile hike. Already she thought of her bedroom as a refuge.

But how could it be a refuge if Karen was going to feel free to barge in at any time?

Karen! Again Nancy felt a pang of guilt. Karen hadn't meant any harm by coming in. She probably had no idea how much Nancy needed a place for privacy in this house.

Nancy brushed away her tears and put the little tiger

down on the bed. She was not proud of the exhibition of temper she had just given. She wondered uneasily if Karen would tell her mother about it—or Mr. Payne. No, she decided, Karen did not seem like a tattletale. She had seemed hurt rather than angered by Nancy's outburst.

Nancy drew a deep breath. It was up to her to put matters right between her stepsister and herself. It wouldn't contribute much to her mother's happiness if Karen and she turned up at the lunch table not speaking to each other.

She opened the door, peered out, and then walked along the little corridor to Karen's open door and knocked gently.

Karen was making her bed. She stopped her vigorous fluffing of a pillow to look at Nancy soberly. Nancy swallowed hard. "Karen—I'm sorry I was such a crab just now—"

"Oh." Karen was as ill at ease as Nancy herself. "I— I had no business to go pawing at your things." There was a wary expression in her blue eyes, as if she expected Nancy to jump at her again any moment.

She thinks I'm a monster! Nancy was surprised to find that she wasn't indifferent to Karen's opinion of her. She heard herself saying, "Truly, I'm not usually as nasty as that."

"I guess it's pretty hard to come to a strange house and suddenly find yourself with a new father and sister," Karen said, with what Nancy felt was surprising perception. "In the future, I'll try not to be a pest."

Remembering again the friendly greeting Karen had

given her upon her arrival, Nancy felt her cheeks grow hot.

"But I'm awfully happy to have you here, Nancy," Karen continued. "I hope we'll be friends. I love your mother already. You see, I can hardly remember my own mother."

Nancy was touched, and all her guards went down. "I'd like to be friends. That is, if you can put up with my horrid disposition."

Karen laughed with a flash of dimples. Nancy guessed that Karen was a girl who laughed and cried easily, but there was a sweetness and honesty about her that was most appealing.

"Come in," Karen invited. "As soon as I've finished tidying up, I'll show you around the house and grounds."

Nancy stepped into the room. It was the same size as her own, but the furniture was ivory-white and the colors were cornflower-blue and daffodil-yellow. An exquisite doll with blond braids was seated on the chintz-cushioned window seat. A record player stood on a low table close by.

"This is Gretchen," Karen said, as Nancy admired the doll. "I've had her forever and I love her to death, even though I'm too old now to play with dolls. So I understand how you feel about your tiger." She turned back to smooth the cornflower-sprigged coverlet on her bed.

"Aunt Florence made me take full care of my room," she explained.

Was this a gentle hint for her to do the same? Nancy wondered. Not that she needed it. She was accustomed to helping with the housework, and she had every intention of pulling her own weight in the Payne household.

She returned to her own room to make her bed and unpack—the suitcase from Vermont and the two other bags and a box of trinkets that her mother had brought from the New York apartment. She was moving about the room, busily putting her things away in drawers and closet, when a roll of several crisp new bills, flung down on the dressing table, caught her eye. Nancy stood still, frowning at the money.

Karen and she had found identical rolls of bills tucked under their plates at the breakfast table that morning. Karen had put hers into the pocket of her blouse with a casual "Thanks, Father." Noting his step-daughter's perplexed expression, Mr. Payne had explained in his hearty manner.

"It's your monthly allowance, Nancy."

Nancy flushed and her green eyes darkened. "Oh! But really, sir, I can't accept all this money."

Her mother looked distressed.

"Nonsense, my dear," Mr. Payne said to Nancy. "You'll need some money, and I expect to provide alike for you and Karen."

His tone implied that the subject of Nancy's allowance was closed. Mrs. Payne's eyes implored her daughter not to make an unpleasant issue of the money, so Nancy had murmured, "Thank you, Mr. Payne. You're very generous."

Now she stared gloomily at the bills. She had accepted Mr. Payne's money to please her mother, but she had no intention of spending any of it. It was bad enough to be forced to be dependent on her stepfather for food and lodging, but money was something different. She would have to find a job to provide some for herself.

For the next few days, Nancy hopefully scanned the "Help Wanted Female" columns of the Glendale Falls *Messenger* for some opening where she might apply. She did not want to baby-sit—she was looking for a steady daytime job—and all the store and office positions had the discouraging word "experienced" in the advertisements.

Nancy decided that she would take a business course when she entered Glendale High School in the fall. Then next summer, she could apply for an office job with some degree of confidence, and by the time she finished high school she'd be able to qualify as an efficient secretary. After her father's death, she had been unhappy because college would be impossible, but today she had only one ambition—to make her own way and be independent of Mr. Payne as soon as possible.

2

Family heirlooms

Mr. Payne took a hearty interest in the everyday doings of his wife and the two girls. Every morning at the breakfast table, he wanted to know how they planned to spend the day, and if they had no plans, he was ready with some suggestions. Nancy resented what she considered his domineering attitude, and it irritated her to see her mother so gently receptive to her husband's advice.

"Better take the girls downtown today and buy them some summer dresses," Mr. Payne said to his wife one morning.

Mrs. Payne and Karen looked pleased at the prospect of a shopping trip. Nancy felt obliged to protest.

"Really, I don't need a thing."

"Nonsense," her stepfather said. "Girls always need new clothes."

He passed his coffee cup to his wife for refilling. "Get them each something pretty for the midsummer banquet of the Museum Associates." He beamed at his family. "We have a fine speaker for the occasion, a famous hunter and explorer." This reminded him of something else. "Karen, take Nancy over to the museum some afternoon and show her around. And while you're there, see how John Craig is coming along with the mounting of Big Black."

Karen nodded, but without much enthusiasm.

Amy Payne loved to shop, and now she was able to spend freely. She treated the two girls to lunch at a charming tearoom and, afterward, they spent hours of lighthearted shopping for summer clothes.

Nancy started out determined not to be a wet blanket on her mother's pleasure, but soon she actually began to enjoy herself. She loved pretty clothes, and she had outgrown all her old ones. For the past three years her clothes allowance had been scarcely enough to buy the essentials, so now it was easy to forget that Mr. Payne was responsible for this shopping trip and to fall in with her mother's happy mood.

Mrs. Payne bought Nancy three new dresses, a skirt and several blouses, party heels and summer flats, and a jade-green cashmere sweater. Her purchases for Karen were equally lavish. Laughing and chattering like three girls together, they walked from the last shop to where their car was parked.

"Father suggested that we drive around before going home," Karen said, "so Nancy can get acquainted with her new home town."

Glendale Falls was a small, prosperous New England

city that had grown up around the tree-shaded campus of Glendale College. Mrs. Payne drove slowly while Karen pointed out the various college buildings.

"You'll be entering Glendale College a year ahead of me," she told Nancy. "We Paynes all go to Glendale."

"But I'm not a Payne," Nancy reminded her. "And perhaps I'll skip college and go to work."

"Father wouldn't hear of it," the younger girl assured her. And she proceeded with her guided tour all unaware that beside her Nancy was seething with rebellion.

"This is the Payne Museum of Natural History," Karen said, as they drove slowly past a large red brick building of colonial design. "It was started by an endowment fund given by my great-grandfather. Now it's famous for its fossil collection and exhibits of the wildlife of eastern North America. The museum is Father's pet." Karen smiled ruefully. "I'm really not much interested in all those dead animals and old bones, but I daren't let Father know."

The Payne house was on the country-club side of town, a park-like residential section. On the opposite side of the city was the industrial section, dominated by the great modern plant occupied by the Payne Toasted Krispys Company.

Nancy had already discovered how important Toasted Krispys were in the Payne household, where large bowls of them were served with sugar and cream every morning.

"Eat your Krispys!" Mr. Payne ordered Nancy almost every morning.

"But there are so many of them," she would protest.

"Krispys are packed with vitamins and nutrition." He plied his own spoon with relish. "And they taste delicious, too." His ruddy face was boyishly eager as he looked at Nancy. "Don't you think they taste good, Nancy?"

"Uh—yes. They taste very good."

Fortunately it was true. Mr. Payne radiated such pride in his product that Nancy would have lacked the courage to pronounce Payne's Krispys anything but good. Still, it made for a monotonous breakfast to have them served every morning. But with Mr. Payne's eyes upon them, his wife and the two girls dutifully ate every Krispy in their cereal bowls.

I suppose I'll have to face up to a bowl of Payne's Krispys every morning of my life until I'm old enough to move out of here, Nancy thought glumly. She giggled as a discouraging idea occurred to her. If she ever married, Mr. Payne's wedding gift would probably be a lifetime supply of Payne's Krispys!

The Sunday after Nancy's arrival in Glendale Falls, Mr. and Mrs. Payne gave a family dinner party, inviting Karen's Aunt Florence Craig, her husband, Professor Craig, and a cousin, Burton Payne.

Knowing how important it was to her mother that she make a good impression on Mr. Payne's relatives, Nancy dressed with special care that day. She was rewarded by her mother's proud smile when she walked into the living room, where the rest of the family had gathered.

She was wearing one of her new dresses, a silky cotton in an old-fashioned red calico print sprigged with black and green. The full skirt and the high neck, with its tiny frill of embroidery, were becoming to her tall, lithe figure. Nancy had not inherited her mother's beauty, and she often mourned over her plain features, but there was an appealing brightness in her expression. Her green eyes, set under dark brows that curved like wings, combined with a soap-and-water complexion to give her charm. She wore her dark hair in a short bob that waved softly about her forehead.

Karen took Nancy affectionately by the hand and led her over to introduce her to Aunt Florence and Professor Craig. Florence Craig gave her brother's stepdaughter a gracious welcome into the family. Her husband, a scholarly looking man, was head of the paleontology department at Glendale College and curator of the Payne Museum.

Burton Payne was introduced last. Karen had already confided that he did not get along well with her father. They had been quarreling for years over the division of their grandmother's estate.

Burton Payne was a bachelor who had retired from business and now devoted his time to painting and to collecting fossils for the Payne Museum. A tall, lanky man dressed in shabby tweeds, and with longish gray-streaked hair, he gave Nancy a friendly greeting as they shook hands. At first impression he seemed an easygoing sort, but Nancy noted how sharp his eyes were behind their dark-rimmed glasses. At dinner, while Oliver Payne was holding forth on his many hunting adventures, Nancy happened to glance at Cousin Burton. There was an almost contemptuous look on his face as he watched Oliver. Nancy decided that Cousin Burton did not like Mr. Payne any better than she herself did.

After dessert, the men went out to the terrace to smoke. Nancy and Karen followed Mrs. Payne and Florence to the kitchen, where Mrs. Payne directed Minnie Bell to find a box or basket in which some dishes could be packed. Then she and Florence started to take an exquisite Wedgwood tea set out of the cupboard in the butler's pantry.

"I'm glad you agree that I'm to have this tea set," Florence said in her pleasant manner, which reminded Nancy of Karen. "It belonged to my mother and grandmother . . ."

"Of course you must have some of the family heirlooms," Mrs. Payne replied cheerfully. "If there's anything else you think you should have, please feel free to take it."

Florence shook her head. "Not so fast! Oliver has definite ideas of what belongs to him and he hangs on to those things."

A sardonic laugh sounded behind them. Burton Payne was standing in the doorway.

"You can say that again, my dear Florence. Oliver isn't noted for letting go of valuables that he gets his hands on. I'm surprised he agreed to let you take the Wedgwood set."

"Burton, I wish you'd stop sulking over Grandmother's necklace," Florence scolded.

"A man has the right to sulk when he's been robbed," Burton snapped.

Mrs. Payne glanced in surprise from one to the other. "You were robbed of your grandmother's jewels, Burton?"

"Robbed indeed. Your . . ."

"Burton!" Florence cried sharply.

Burton shrugged his shoulders and made the new Mrs. Payne a little bow. 'Forgive me, Cousin Amy, for rattling the bones of the family skeleton. I have to leave now. Many thanks for a most delicious dinner."

"Come again soon," she said cordially, giving him her hand.

As Burton took his leave, Florence Craig murmured, "I wish I knew the true story of that necklace."

Mrs. Payne's curiosity had been aroused. When they joined Mr. Payne and Professor Craig on the terrace, she sat down beside her husband. "What's all this about someone robbing Burton of your grandmother's necklace?" she asked.

Mr. Payne jumped as if a firecracker had suddenly exploded under his chair. His ruddy color deepened.

"Oh, my," Karen murmured in Nancy's ear, "any allusion to Cousin Burton and that necklace is enough to send Father into orbit."

"What's that idiot Burton been telling you?" Mr. Payne demanded angrily of his wife.

"Why—he only hinted that he'd been robbed." She looked surprised and dismayed by her husband's violent reaction to her remark.

"What Burton was hinting at is that I'm the thief," Mr. Payne told her bluntly.

"Oliver!" she cried, shocked. "Where is the necklace now?"

"In my safe-deposit box." He sounded smugly triumphant. "And just let Burton try to get his hands on it."

Mrs. Payne glanced helplessly at her sister-in-law. Florence shrugged and then said, "Let's change this unpleasant subject."

Professor Craig tried to oblige. "Our stegosaurus is nicely mounted and will go on display at the museum this week," he announced happily.

This bit of information only served to irritate Mr. Payne. "John, you've been neglecting the Big Black exhibit in order to get that stegosaurus of yours and Burton's mounted before the Associates' banquet!" he scolded. "Now I want Big Black ready before the midsummer banquet. You understand me?"

"I understand you, Oliver," the professor replied wearily. "I've already assured you that your bear will be ready."

"It had better be," Mr. Payne grumbled. "I want to see Hank Rawlings' face when he finds himself looking at the biggest black bear he ever saw in his life."

"Let's take a walk," Karen whispered to Nancy. "I can tell that Father is getting ready to tell how he shot Big Black, and we all know the story by heart."

They descended the three steps set into the stone wall of the terrace and strolled through a flower garden where roses filled the air with fragrance. Nancy reflected that she had indeed come to live in a lovely place.

"Who is Hank Rawlings?" she asked. "Why is your father in such a flurry about impressing him? And who or what is Big Black?"

"It's easy to tell that you haven't been around our house long." Karen sighed. "Big Black is a huge bear that Father shot last year in Maine. And Mr. Rawlings is a famous big-game hunter who is going to be guest speaker at the midsummer banquet. Big Black is being mounted for the Wildlife Hall, and Father wants to be sure it will be in its place when he takes Mr. Rawlings on a tour of the museum."

So he can boast of shooting a poor wild creature, who was minding its own business in the Maine woods until Oliver Payne came along with his gun, Nancy thought with a shiver of distaste.

The two girls sat down on a stone bench hidden from the terrace by a clump of arborvitae.

"I'm just bursting with curiosity today," Nancy confessed. "Now I want to know all about your great-grandmother's mysterious necklace."

"It's set with topazes that glitter like sunbursts," Karen told her. "It's very beautiful and not really mysterious, although it *has* caused plenty of trouble. Father and Cousin Burton have been fighting about that necklace for years. You see, Great-grandmother Payne lived to be almost a hundred. She had some beautiful jewelry and she left it all to Father and Aunt Florence in her will. She was angry with Cousin Burton because he'd refused to marry the girl she'd picked out for him."

Bossy as her grandson Oliver, was the tag Nancy mentally pinned on Great-grandmother Payne.

"But shortly before she died, Great-grandmother made up her quarrel with Burton," Karen continued. "Burton claims that she intended to change her will in his favor, and that in his presence she told Father that Burton was to have the topaz necklace, her most valuable piece of jewelry. Then she died before the will could be changed. Father has always denied the part about the necklace. According to him, Great-grandmother said that Burton was to have a piece of her jewelry, but that Father, as executor of her will, was to decide which piece it should be. Father offered Burton a pair of diamond bracelets when the estate was settled, but Burton refused them in a perfect fury. He wanted that necklace, but Father wanted it just as much, and Father usually succeeds in getting what he wants."

Nancy felt a stirring of sympathy for Cousin Burton.

"If the necklace is so valuable, Burton probably feels that he needs it more than your father does."

Karen gave a peal of laughter. "Don't let Cousin Burton's old tweed suit and ancient car deceive you. He has as much money as Father. It's Burton who finances Professor Craig's—Uncle John's—fossil-hunting expeditions. They've been buddies ever since they were boys. I guess that's one reason Father was against Aunt Florence marrying Professor Craig. He wouldn't even go to the wedding, but he let me go. I was Aunt Florence's bridesmaid, and Cousin Burton was best man. Afterward, Father relented and sent them a handsome wedding present. He loves Aunt Florence dearly, and it hurt him to lose her."

Nancy sniffed. Oliver Payne had taken a queer way of showing that he loved his sister. He wants to manage the lives of everyone around him, she thought. But he's not going to manage mine!

"Hi, Barry! Hi, Ruthie!" Karen called suddenly, waving to a girl and boy who had pushed through the hemlock hedge dividing the Payne property from the house next door. They waved back and walked across the lawn to join Karen and Nancy. The girl, chubby in her white dress, with red bows tying her fair pigtails, looked to be about nine. Her companion was a jaunty teen-age boy with a good-humored face topped by curly, close-cropped hair. In one hand the girl was carrying a small turtle.

"How come you're home from your grandmother's?" Karen demanded. "I thought you were staying three weeks."

"Oh, Mom began to worry about Dad not getting regular meals," the boy replied.

Karen introduced them to Nancy as their next door neighbors and her oldest friends, Barry and Ruthie Webster.

"And this is my new sister, Nancy Frost," she added with a beaming smile.

Ruthie smiled shyly. Barry gave Nancy's hand a warm shake.

"Mom almost flipped when she heard that your old man had married again," he told Karen with easy candor.

"I didn't even know myself until he brought my new mother home. But she couldn't be nicer."

"So your aunt told Mom. Mom is going to call on her soon," Barry assured the girls.

At this point, the turtle began to wave its sturdy legs. Slowly and carefully, Ruthie set it down on the grass.

"Where did you get the turtle, Ruthie?" Karen asked.

"In the woods near Grandmother's house."

"Nothing would do but that she must drag the poor critter home with her," Barry added.

"Violet would have felt bad if I had left her behind," Ruthie said calmly. "She likes me."

She pulled a wilted lettuce leaf from her skirt pocket and dropped down on the grass to offer it to the turtle. Violet accepted the tidbit and crushed it between beak-like jaws in seeming contentment. Nancy joined Ruthie and the turtle. Although she had never been allowed to keep a pet in their city apartment, she loved animals and always enjoyed the company of Aunt Kathy's cats, her setter dog, and the farm animals.

"Violet is a sort of odd-looking turtle," she remarked. "Her shell is so bumpy."

The painted turtles and snapping turtles who inhabited the old millpond near her aunt's place in Vermont all had comparatively smooth shells, but Violet's was dome-shaped and its brown and yellow plates were sculptured into little pyramids.

"She's really very handsome," Nancy decided.

"Violet is a wood turtle," Ruthie explained. She regarded her pet fondly while Violet stared back with

beady eyes that seemed to mirror the wisdom of the
ages. "I looked her up in a nature book at the library.
She can swim if she wants to, and at mating time she'll
go to a brook or pond to meet a boy turtle, but she
spends most of her time on land. In winter she digs herself down into the ground to hibernate."

"For Pete's sake," said Barry, "do you think we want
to listen to a lecture on that stupid turtle?"

"I think Violet is very interesting," Nancy said.

The turtle had started to crawl across the grass in
search of more food. "Let's go and see if Violet would
like a rosebud to eat," Nancy suggested to Ruthie.

Ruthie scooped up Violet and walked companiona-
bly beside Nancy to the rose garden. Karen and Barry
stayed behind on the bench beneath the arborvitaes.
Karen had talked a lot about the boy next door, and
Nancy suspected that she would not take it amiss to be
left alone with him.

After Ruthie went home to put Violet in her pen,
Nancy returned to the house. The company had left.
Mr. Payne was napping on a chaise longue in a shady
corner of the terrace. Inside, the big house had a Sunday
afternoon quiet. Mrs. Payne was resting in her room.

In the living room, the Sunday paper lay on a table.
Nancy looked for the classified advertising section and
carried it up to her room. Hopefully she scanned the columns headed "Help Wanted Female." The first advertisements she read were disappointing, but halfway
down the column she came on one that made her heart
beat a little faster.

WANTED: High school girl to assist in Museum Shop and do some typing. Moderate pay but interesting work. See Miss May Monday morning. 200 Elm Street. (Next door to the Payne Museum.)

An eager little smile curved Nancy's mouth as she re-read the advertisement. "Interesting work" sounded good, and that hateful word "experience" had been left out. She could type fairly well. Oh, she was going to try for this one!

She copied the address carefully and tucked the slip of paper into her clutch bag. Then she carried the paper back to the living room. Job hunting was going to be her secret until she could come home and announce that she was a paid employee.

3

A new job

The following morning Minnie Bell gave Mrs. Payne a long list of groceries to be bought, and Mrs. Payne invited the two girls to accompany her to the supermarket. Karen accepted with enthusiasm.

"I just love to browse along the shelves of a market," she declared. "It's like going on a treasure hunt."

Nancy's lips curved in a wry smile. Karen would not have found anything exciting or adventuresome in the penny-pinching marketing that Nancy and her mother had done while they were on their own.

"I'm sorry I can't go with you this morning, Mother," she said. "I have a project of my own that needs doing."

"Oh?" Her mother looked disappointed. "Might one ask what this project is?"

Nancy shook her head. "It's a secret for a while."

Her mother laughed. One of her finer points in Nancy's eyes was that she never pried. She knew Nancy would eventually come to her to discuss anything of importance.

Karen was different. "What's this mysterious project? Can't it wait until afternoon?"

"No," Nancy replied shortly.

She was not happy about keeping her plan to get a job secret from her mother, but if Mother told Oliver Payne about it, he might try to keep Nancy from carrying out the project. He seemed to be opposed to having anyone in his family be even the least bit independent.

Nancy's heart gave an odd lurch as she watched her mother and Karen drive away together. Even though she was becoming genuinely fond of Karen, it was hard to share her mother with another girl. She tried not to be jealous, but still there was the feeling of having lost something that had been exclusively her own.

As soon as the car had disappeared down the drive, she ran upstairs to change her clothes. She put on her new green corduroy skirt, a white blouse with dainty tucks, but not too dressy to wear in applying for a job, and her jade-green sweater. Taking her clutch bag, she hurried down to the basement, where Minnie Bell was chatting with the woman who came in to do the laundry.

"Thought you had gone to market with your ma," Minnie said in surprise.

"No. I'm doing something on my own this morning. Can you tell me when the next bus goes past the foot of our road?"

Minnie glanced at the electric clock. "There's a bus due in five minutes."

"Oh, I'll have to hurry. Please tell Mother that I've

gone to town on an errand and that I'll be back in time for lunch."

Minnie looked after her with a puzzled expression. The housekeeper was plainly bursting with curiosity about what the new daughter of the house was up to.

Nancy ran most of the way down winding Orchard Road to its junction with the highway. To her relief, she reached the bus stop just as the bus itself appeared around a curve up the road. She would have hated to have her mother and Karen come back and find her waiting for the bus.

A question to the driver established the fact that she could leave the bus only a block away from the museum on Elm Street. She sat clutching her purse tightly, worrying lest some earlier applicant might get the job before she could reach the May house. When at last she was walking along Elm Street, she told herself that it was silly to be so tense and nervous. People applied for positions every day—and often got them, too!

Huge wineglass elms shaded the street and cast dappled shadows on the white pillars and rose brick walls of the Payne Museum. Behind the museum stretched the green turf of the Glendale College campus, shady with oaks and elms and edged by ivy-covered buildings.

On Elm Street, just beyond the Museum and separated from it by a narrow stretch of lawn and a white picket fence, stood a small white house with green blinds. Nancy paused at the gate and glanced at the house number. A flagstone walk led to the front door with its side lights of old, bubbly, greenish glass. Beside

the door, a wooden plaque stated that this was the Elias
May house, built in 1774. It was a darling little house
and it looked exactly as the home of someone named
Miss May should look.

Nancy stood there for several minutes before she
summoned the courage to push the gate open. She
stepped quickly along the walk between clumps of violet leaves and blossoming coral bells, mounted the two
low steps, and gave the polished brass knocker a thud.
The door opened immediately.

"I saw you out on the walk," a musical voice said.
"And I hoped you were coming in."

"Miss May?" Nancy asked doubtfully.

In her mind, she had pictured how a woman who
lived in this delightful house and had such a charming
name should look: a birdlike, pink-cheeked person with
fluffy silvery hair. The handsome woman in the doorway could scarcely have been more different. She was a
rather large person, wearing a blue denim blouse and
a wrap-around skirt. Her dark hair was streaked with
gray at the temples. Her mouth was humorous but firm,
her hazel eyes very bright and direct. Only her beautiful voice went with Nancy's image.

"Yes, I'm Annie May," she replied with a welcoming
smile.

"I'm Nancy Frost. I . . ."

"I hope you've come in answer to my ad," Miss May
finished for her. "Come in."

She ushered Nancy through a little hall and into a
long living room full of old-time charm and homey comfort. Flowered curtains hung at the many-paned win-

dows. There was a tile fireplace with a pair of haughty white-and-gold Staffordshire cats seated on the mantelpiece, and on either side, floor-to-ceiling shelves were crammed with books. Nancy did not know much about period furniture, but many of the pieces had a mellow glow that made her judge them to be antiques. Miss May sat down on the sofa and motioned Nancy to a seat in a wing chair nearby.

"You did come about the ad, didn't you?" she asked a little anxiously. Nancy nodded. "Good! You're the fourth this morning, and I was beginning to believe that no one at all suitable was going to show up. One of the girls who came was wearing shorts! And another looked as though she were made up for a TV horror picture. Not that I'm averse to sports attire in its proper sphere or to a touch of make-up delicately applied," she added hastily.

"My mother turns thumbs down on anything but a little lipstick," Nancy told her.

Miss May nodded, well pleased. "When I saw you at the gate, you looked, well, exactly like the kind of girl I want for an assistant. I said to myself, 'There she is!' And then I thought you'd never come to the door!"

They laughed together.

"Ah, Smilodon," Miss May said, "come in and meet our visitor."

A large golden tiger cat walked proudly into the room and padded over to rub against Miss May. His amber eyes studied Nancy seriously, as if he were evaluating her.

"Kitty?" Nancy murmured, holding out her h a gesture of friendship.

After a moment, the cat went to her. Nancy .... him gently behind his ears, in the spot where Aunt Kathy's cats loved to be caressed. Smilodon liked it, too. A deep, rumbling purr started in his throat, and he arched his furry head hard against her hand.

"There! Smilodon has accepted you," Miss May exclaimed, as if that cinched the matter. "I'd trust his judgment before I'd trust my own. He wouldn't even come into the room with those other girls."

Nancy smiled gratefully at Smilodon. "He doesn't look or act like a saber-toothed tiger."

"So you know something about prehistoric animals." Miss May looked pleased.

Nancy nodded. "When I was about ten, I used to eat up books about dinosaurs and the beasts of the tar pits. And I'll never forget that saber-tooth stalking the cavemen in Jack London's *Before Adam*."

"More and more you seem just the helper I've been looking for! But of course you want to know what your duties will be."

Nancy sat forward eagerly.

"I keep a little shop over in the museum," Miss May explained. "And now Professor Craig has asked me to give talks on the exhibits to groups of children, women's clubs, and so forth, who visit the museum. Do you think you'd be interested in being my assistant?"

"I'd love it! But—I don't know how I'd be at giving talks."

"You'll have to trail along with me a few times and study the exhibits, of course, and do some reading up on them. I'll help you write a little lecture. The typing I mentioned in the advertisement won't be much—just orders for the shop and a few business letters."

"I'm not a fast typist," Nancy warned her.

"You needn't be fast so long as you're neat and accurate. Now about money . . ." Miss May mentioned a modest salary. "And your hours will be from twelve-thirty until five-thirty. The museum opens at one and closes at five, and then we must close the shop. You'll have Sundays and Mondays off. The shop is closed on Sunday, and the entire museum is closed on Monday. Well, Nancy Frost, does the job appeal to you?"

"Oh, it does! It does!" Nancy's voice rang with delight. If she had searched the world over, she could not have found work more to her liking.

"Good." Miss May seemed equally satisfied. "I'm sure that we'll get on well together. Now perhaps you would like to tell me something about yourself. To begin with, where do you live?"

"I'm new in Glendale Falls. Oliver Payne is my stepfather. Perhaps you know him?"

"Know him!" Miss May exclaimed. "Goodness me. So you're Oliver Payne's stepdaughter! Well, I am surprised. Did you know that this is the Payne Museum next door?"

Nancy nodded.

"Does Oliver know that you're applying for work there?"

"No." Nancy decided to be frank. "I didn't want

to say anything at home until I got the job. I was afraid that Mr. Payne might prefer to have me just play around all summer with Karen. But you see, I want to earn my own spending money."

"Hmm." Miss May looked thoughtful but sympathetic. "And how about your mother?"

"When I tell her tonight, I'm sure Mother will give her permission for me to come to work for you." Nancy tensed in sudden alarm. "Miss May, will the fact that I'm Mr. Payne's stepdaughter keep me from getting the job?"

"Not if you can get permission at home to work at the museum. You go home and talk to your mother—then telephone me. If your mother approves, you may start tomorrow."

As Nancy left the May house, she heard the chug of a power lawn mower. A tall boy in blue jeans was cutting the stretch of lawn between the Museum and the picket fence. He had thick dark hair and a sun-tanned face. He certainly wasn't a handsome boy, but as she walked along Elm Street, something about him made Nancy steal a second glance. To her surprise, the boy was looking at her! He grinned and raised one hand in greeting. Nancy's cheeks grew pink, but she smiled shyly and hurried on, walking with a free stride.

Boys did not often notice her, maybe because she was too tall and too plain of face. This boy must be working on the college maintenance force. She wondered what his name was and whether she would get to know him when she went to work for Miss May.

When Nancy arrived home, she was glad to find that

Karen was upstairs, washing her hair in preparation for a date with Barry Webster that evening.

"I had begun to worry, Nancy," Mrs. Payne chided her. "Where have you been all morning?"

Nancy took her mother's arm and drew her into the living room. "Let's sit here on the sofa, Mother, where we can talk by ourselves. I have so much to tell you. I have a job!"

"A job!" Her mother looked at her in amazement. "You went out looking for a job without saying anything to me! Where is this job? And why do you want a job?"

"I want to earn my own spending money for one thing."

Nancy felt a prickle of exasperation. Her mother ought to realize how she felt about the spending money without being told.

"Don't you see, Mother? I just can't depend on Mr. Payne for everything."

"No, I do not see!" Mrs. Payne said sharply. "Nancy, I haven't talked to you before about this, but I feel that you hurt Oliver by your stand-offish attitude toward him. He's tried in every way to show you that he wants to be a kind, indulgent father."

Nancy's green eyes blazed. "But he's not my father! I don't want his kindness. I don't want anything from him! I hate . . ."

She broke off at the sight of her mother's pale, shocked face.

"I didn't realize that you were hiding such feelings," Mrs. Payne said in a strained voice.

Nancy bit her lip. Why, oh, why, couldn't she learn to control her temper? She always ended by hurting other people and putting herself in the wrong.

"Forgive me, Mother. I—I sounded worse than I really feel." She put her arm around her mother and kissed her. "I want you to be happy. And I'm trying awfully hard to like Mr. Payne."

"I don't understand why you have to try so hard," her mother answered, sighing. "Oliver is a fine man, a generous and affectionate man. Believe me, Nancy, in spite of what my own feelings might have been, I never would have married him if I hadn't been quite sure that it was best for you, too. Don't this lovely home and the many advantages that Oliver is able and eager to give you mean anything at all?"

Nancy glanced around the comfortable, beautiful room. "It certainly is much more pleasant here than in our New York flat," she admitted. Determined to be completely honest, she added, "I do enjoy having nice clothes and—and everything. But I—I—oh, I guess I'm just plain jealous."

"Oh, darling," her mother cried reproachfully. "Have I changed in the least toward you? Have I?"

"No, no. That's not what I meant." Nancy didn't add that she just could not bear to have anyone in Daddy's place. She drew a deep breath, half sigh and half sob. "Perhaps if I had a job, and could be a little independent, I'd feel differently toward Mr. Payne."

Her mother, too, gave a little sigh. "Well, tell me about this position that means so much to you."

Nancy began to talk eagerly about Miss May and her

charming old house and what the work at the Museum would be. Her eyes sparkled and her face glowed with enthusiasm.

"It does sound like a fascinating place to work," Mrs. Payne said at last. "But Oliver will never be able to understand why you want to do to it. He wants you and Karen to enjoy your summer."

Nancy fought down an impulse to cry out that she didn't care what Oliver Payne wanted and didn't see why he should be consulted.

"I will be enjoying the summer in my own way. Please let me take the job, Mother. Call Miss May now —before Karen comes downstairs," she urged.

Mrs. Payne noted Nancy's tense hands and pleading eyes. "Very well," she said after a moment. "Since your heart is set on it, I'll telephone your Miss May."

"I'll look up the number!"

Nancy dashed into the hall and thumbed wildly through the telephone book. Then she sat on the stairs and listened while her mother made the call and chatted with Miss May. Finally Mrs. Payne put the telephone down and turned to Nancy with a smile.

"Well, dear, it's all settled. You start work tomorrow. Miss May wants you to come for lunch, about twelve, so that she'll have time to show you the shop before the museum opens."

"Whee!" Nancy seized her mother around the waist and whirled her around the hall in jig time until they both collapsed in a storm of laughter on the bottom steps of the graceful Georgian staircase.

"What in the world goes on here?" Karen, her tawny hair rolled up on pink curlers, came running down the stairs.

"I've got a job is what's going on," Nancy caroled. "I'm going to work for Miss May at the Museum."

Karen looked utterly flabbergasted. "Why ever do you want to get a stupid old job?" she asked reproachfully. "I thought we'd be having such fun together this summer."

"There'll still be time for fun," Nancy assured her.

A pixie grin lighted Karen's pretty face. "This is going to be an awful shock to Father, coming right after Mother made him agree to let Barry and me go to the movies on our own in Barry's car. Until now, Father always insisted on driving us to the theater and picking us up again after the show, as if we belonged to the kindergarten set."

"Your father believes in taking good care of you," Mrs. Payne said. "Don't forget, you're still only fourteen. But Barry is a nice boy and an old friend; I'm sure he'll get you home safely before your curfew time."

Karen hesitated a moment. Then she said, "Will you come to the movies with us tonight, Nancy?"

Nancy shook her head, smiling. She wasn't going to be a third on Karen's date.

"Thanks—but of course I won't go. Barry wants to date *you.*"

"It doesn't seem right to leave you home alone."

"Now listen here, Karen," Nancy said crisply, "I'm not a guest here. I'm a member of the family. There'll be lots of times when one of us will be going out without the other." It was a good time to establish this, for her own sake as well as Karen's.

Nothing was said to Mr. Payne about Nancy's job until Karen had departed happily with Barry. Karen's father saw them off with warnings to Barry to drive carefully and come right home after the movie.

"But we want to stop at the Corner Shop for a soda," Karen protested.

Mr. Payne glanced helplessly over his shoulder at his wife. When she nodded, he told Karen, "Make it a brief stop then. I want you home before eleven."

Karen blew her family a kiss as Barry started the car.

Nancy took a book and went out on the terrace. Soon Mr. Payne stepped through one of the French windows opening from the living room. He took a chair near Nancy's and studied her with a puzzled expression.

"Your mother tells me that you want to go to work," he said abruptly.

"Yes, sir."

A frown creased the big man's forehead. "Why don't you call me 'Father?'" he asked. "I've asked you to often enough. It embarrassed me yesterday to have you call me Mr. Payne before Florence and Burton."

Nancy was surprised to find herself feeling a little guilty because she could not oblige him. But "Father" was not a term to be lightly bestowed, and she could not imagine herself ever giving it to Oliver Payne.

"It—it takes a little time," she murmured, looking down at her book.

"I suppose so," he conceded with a sigh. He shook his head, as if his new stepdaughter bewildered him. "About this position as Annie May's assistant. I don't approve, Nancy. Why aren't you willing to stay home and enjoy yourself with Karen? Later in the summer, I plan to take the whole family for a trip. Anything you want or need anytime, I'll be more than glad to give to you."

"You're very generous, Mr. Payne, but what I want and need most is a little independence—like earning my own spending money."

"I am continuing your allowance whether you go to work or not," he said quickly.

They looked at each other, each pair of eyes stubborn and unflinching. After a moment Mr. Payne let out a sigh that sounded almost like a groan.

"You're so unlike my gentle little Karen that I'm hard put to understand you, Nancy. But very well, if nothing else will make you happy, I'd rather have you working at the museum than anywhere else."

Nancy was reading in bed when Karen returned from her date, dimpled and happy. She peeked around the door and then came in to perch at the foot of the bed. Nancy held up the *Guide to the Payne Museum of Natural History*.

"I found this in the bookcase and I've been doing my homework."

"Oh, that silly job!" Karen sniffed. "I suppose if I want to see you after tomorrow, I'll have to come down and dig around in a lot of dinosaurs."

Nancy chuckled. "Was the movie good?"

"It was dreamy. Next time we go, Barry will find a date for you."

"That's good of him," Nancy said without enthusiasm.

She didn't want Karen's boyfriend finding dates for her, any more than she wanted Karen's father providing her with spending money.

"Oh, Nancy," Karen went on happily, "I have such a wonderful idea. My birthday is Friday and I'm going to ask Mother if I can have a party—a cookout. It will be a grand opportunity for you to get acquainted with some of the crowd you'll be meeting at school next fall."

"You'll get me launched in society in spite of myself." Nancy laughed, finding Karen's high spirits contagious. "Mother will be delighted to fall in with your plans. She loves parties, and for a long time there was nary a party in our lives."

The boy at the museum

When Nancy knocked on Miss May's door near noon the next day, she was surprised to have it opened by the tall boy who had been mowing the lawn on Monday.

"Hello, Nancy Frost," he greeted her. "Come in. Miss May is in the kitchen preparing lunch. I'm Alan Shelby, and I'm pleased indeed to meet you." He gave her a friendly grin.

Alan showed Nancy to the kitchen, a bright room with windows on two sides. Miss May stood at the counter making ham salad sandwiches. She gave Nancy a cordial welcome and asked her to be seated.

"I'm so glad your mother agreed to let you come to work for me. How did Oliver take it?" she asked, her hazel eyes twinkling.

Nancy laughed. "Well—I'm here."

She sat down in one of the captain's chairs around a table by the windows. Between crisp cottage curtains she glimpsed a garden and a shady stretch of lawn. There were flowering shrubs along the picket fence that surrounded Miss May's entire property and cut it off from the campus. It seemed odd that just this one dwelling should stand here almost on the college grounds.

As if sensing her visitor's thoughts, Miss May said, "We Mays were here long before the college. Most of the college buildings stand on land that was part of our farm in Revolutionary days. Now I'm glad to eke out a living by working at the museum."

Alan Shelby seemed to be very much at home in this kitchen. While Miss May filled three green pottery bowls from a kettle of soup heating on the stove, Alan carried the plate of sandwiches to the table, filled a sugar bowl at the cannister on the counter, and brought three saucers of ripe red strawberries and a jug of cream from the refrigerator.

It came out in the conversation during lunch that Alan was seventeen, that he had another year of high school ahead of him, and that he lived in a Maine mill town. He had come to Glendale Falls looking for work to help swell his college fund, having heard of the town from sportsmen who had stayed at his uncle's fishing and hunting camp in Maine. Since Alan had no place to stay, the head of the college employment bureau had asked Miss May whether she would rent him the little room over her kitchen. When Alan came to look at the room, Miss May had liked him at once, and she had suggested that he take his meals with her. He had been at the May house for almost a week now, and the two were getting along famously.

The maintenance department was short-staffed, and Alan had been kept too busy mowing lawns, trimming hedges, and planting ornamental shrubs around the college buildings to have time for much else, but he revealed that he was especially interested in seeing the exhibits of the wildlife of eastern North America for which the Payne Museum was famous.

"I'll drop in someday and you can show me through the museum," he said to Nancy. "Is it a date?"

She nodded with a pleased little smile, feeling that Alan was perhaps the most interesting boy she had ever met. She seemed able to talk to him easily, although she was usually shy with boys, and she liked the clean look of his dark skin and straight black hair, which had a jaunty way of falling over his forehead. His eyes were gray, clear, and direct, and all his features were strongly chiseled.

Sitting in the cozy kitchen with Alan and Miss May, Nancy felt more at home than at any time since coming to Glendale Falls.

After lunch, Alan started to help clear the table; then he glanced at the clock, let out a "Yips!" and dashed for the door.

"Thanks for the good lunch, Miss May," he called back, as the screen door banged behind him. "I'll be seeing you, Nancy!"

"He's a fine boy," Miss May said, watching through the window as he loped across the grass toward one of the more distant college buildings. "But somehow I have the feeling that he hasn't told the full story of what brought him to Glendale."

Escorted by Smilodon, Miss May and Nancy walked to the museum, going around to the front of the building. An elderly man in an Oxford-gray uniform was just unlocking the heavy front door. Miss May introduced him as Mr. Baron, the caretaker.

They entered a spacious hall. A marble staircase went up at one side, and wide doorways opened on corridors and an exhibition hall. Miss May's little shop occupied the space in front of one of the high windows that flanked the doorway. In front of the other window with its small, leaded panes were a chair, a desk, and a telephone for Mr. Baron. A closed door marked the office of the curator.

With the familiarity of one who had spent many hours there, Smilodon padded into the shop and leaped onto the sill of the big window, which looked out on the stately white columns of the museum portico. Beneath the window stood a table with a roll of wrapping paper and bins containing bags and boxes for merchandise. The shop was walled on either side by shelves filled with books on Indians, minerals, and natural history. Across the front stretched a large glass showcase, and in this there were small ceramic and carved wood figures of birds, animals, and dinosaurs, as well as ceramic, silver, and enameled jewelry.

Nancy listened carefully while Miss May explained about the stock, quoted prices, and unlocked the money drawer, into which she put change and bills. She locked the drawer again and glanced across to see if Mr. Baron was at his desk.

"I just have time to show Nancy around the halls, Mr. Baron. Will you keep an eye on the shop while we're away?"

He nodded and looked at his watch. "I'll be opening in twenty minutes, though," he said.

Miss May led Nancy toward a wide doorway that faced the shop across the entrance hall.

"I'll take you through quickly, but later, whenever things are quiet at the shop, I want you to stroll through the halls and familiarize yourself with the exhibits. To-day we'll both be in the shop. Tomorrow I have two talks to make to visiting groups, and I want you to come along to get pointers for your own talk. Mr. Baron will tend shop while we're away. By next week I'll expect you to alternate with me at keeping shop and conducting tours through the lower rooms of the museum."

"I hope I'll be ready by then," Nancy said nervously. "Do we go upstairs, too?"

Miss May shook her head. "Our activities are confined to the Hall of Dinosaurs and the Wildlife Hall down here on the first floor. Upstairs are the Indian rooms and the mineral exhibits, and there's a young man to look after things there."

While she was talking, they entered the high, vast Hall of the Dinosaurs. The first thing that caught Nancy's eyes was the upended skeleton of an enormous turtle standing against the wall not far from the door. It was at least ten feet high—big enough to make the largest turtle swimming in the modern seas look like a pigmy. Nancy tipped her head back to get a better view.

"I wonder if Ruthie Webster has ever seen this monster," she murmured.

Supported by metal plates and rods, the ancient turtle skeleton was decorative in a stupendous way. Its long bony flippers spread out starlike, and the framework of its shells formed a strong, clean design.

"This is Archelon, the great turtle who lived in our Middle West during the Cretaceous period of the earth's history, when a warm sea covered the central part of North America," Miss May explained. "Children are invariably interested in turtles and they ask lots of questions, so be prepared, Nancy!"

On the wall beside Archelon was a mural showing the giant turtle disporting himself in the Cretaceous sea. Pterodactyls skimmed the waves on their enormous wings. In the background, the sinister head of Mosasaurus, the predatory sea-serpent lizard, showed above the waves, its baleful eyes watching Archelon. Nancy studied the mural, enthralled. How had the drama of prehistoric times ended? Had Archelon managed to slip away from the sea serpent and hide in the mud at the bottom of the sea? Had some upheaval of nature caused him to die in his hiding place, so that his fossilized bones could be dug up by paleontologists millions of years later?

"Enthralling, isn't it?" said Miss May beside her. She gave Nancy's arm a tug. "But come along. There's a lot to see in a short time."

They strolled through the great hall. Miss May pointed out some dinosaur tracks in slabs of stone that had been found in the Connecticut River valley. On the wall next to them was the skeleton outline of the bones of a tyrannosaurus, the ferocious carnivorous dinosaur, set in plaster and towering to the ceiling.

"Someday we hope to have a complete tyrannosaurus

skeleton," said Miss May. "Burton Payne and Professor Craig are already planning their next fossil-hunting expedition. There stands the fruit of the last one!" She waved her arm.

Standing in awesome splendor at the end of the hall was the newly-mounted skeleton of a stegosaurus. The giant armored reptile was braced on its broad feet and pillarlike legs as firmly as it must have stood while browsing among the lush grasses and ferns of far-off Jurassic time. A double row of large plates made an exotic flare along the top of its backbone. Its long tail was armed with four spikes to be used as a possible means of defense.

"It's overwhelming!" breathed Nancy. "What condition of nature could have been responsible for such a freakish monster?"

"You'll have to ask Professor Craig about that." Miss May gazed proudly at the grotesque skeleton. "There's not one bone missing. Burton Payne and John Craig gave our museum a tremendous boost when they brought back this gem from their last expedition to the West."

Behind the skeleton, on the back wall of the hall, a large mural was in the process of being painted. It showed a stegosaurus and contemporary animals grazing and browsing amid luxuriant Jurassic lowlands with volcanoes smoking in the background. A tall thin man in paint-splashed coveralls was standing on a scaffold working on the mural. At the sound of their voices, he looked around, then put down his paintbrush and turned to face them.

"Hello, Annie," he called down.

The artist was Burton Payne. Miss May smiled at him.

"Burton, your stegosaurus is the most wonderful thing that ever happened to this museum."

He chuckled. "Better not let Cousin Oliver hear you say that. Aren't you overlooking Big Black and all those racks of animal heads and horns that my esteemed cousin has lavished on this institution?"

Suddenly he took a second look at Nancy and seemed to realize for the first time who she was.

"Hello, Nancy," he greeted her pleasantly. "It didn't take you long to find your way here. How do you like our museum?"

"Your stegosaurus leaves me breathless, Mr. Payne," Nancy replied. "I'd hate to meet the likes of him walking in the woods. And this mural is just beautiful," she added. She was astonished to discover that Burton Payne was an accomplished artist.

He looked pleased. "Call me Cousin Burton, my dear, as Karen does."

"Thank you. I will."

Nancy found something interesting and likable about this gray-haired man whose sharp eyes were twinkling at her from behind his glasses. It was hard to think of him as a close relative of bombastic Oliver Payne.

"You'll be seeing Nancy here often," said Miss May. "She's my new helper in the shop. She answered my ad in the paper."

Burton Payne looked astonished. "I admire your initiative, but how did you manage to get Oliver's permission to go to work? He's always kept Karen caged up like a pretty bird."

"My *mother* said I could come to work here," Nancy told him stiffly.

"Come, Nancy, we must finish our walk before the museum opens," Miss May said.

"And I had better get out of here before I have a dozen little modern monsters trying to help me paint," said Burton.

Miss May and Nancy turned into a broad corridor where Nancy saw the bones and restored figures of other prehistoric mammals who had dominated the earth after the age of the giant reptiles had passed. This corridor opened into another large hall that was lined on both sides with glass cases, some filled with mounted birds and others showing habitat groups of the wild animals of eastern North America against artfully designed backgrounds.

Looking into the cases, Nancy found it easy to imagine herself standing in the autumn woods, or in a spruce swamp, or on a rocky mountainside. The large-as-life trees and bushes looked real. There were birds and squirrels in the branches. The ground in one case was covered with scarlet, russet, and golden autumn leaves. In the next case it was spring, and delicate hepaticas and bloodroot were pushing up amid the rocks and dry leaves. A raccoon was fishing for frogs along the edge of a moonlit woodland pond. A red fox was stalking a partridge in the autumn woods. A lynx was sunning herself outside her den, with her kittens playing on the rocky ledge beside her. Next to the lynx was an empty case.

"This is where Big Black will be displayed," said Miss May. "Oliver has given most of this wildlife collection to the museum, and when the bear is in its place the collection will be complete."

"It seems strange that Mr. Payne should be so interested in the modern wildlife exhibits, while his cousin only cares about the prehistoric animals," Nancy remarked, as they walked on along the corridor that brought them back to the entrance hall.

"They are rivals in the museum as they have been in other matters. Both are wealthy men, and both have been generous in their contributions, but most of the staff and the Museum Associates feel that Burton's work has been more outstanding. We would have preferred to have Burton or Professor Craig for the speaker at our midsummer banquet, to give us the highlights of their noteworthy trip, when they dug up the stegosaurus, but Oliver absolutely insisted that Mr. Rawlings be invited instead. Of course we all know it's because he's jealous of Burton . . ."

She broke off suddenly and a faint flush crept into her cheeks.

"I'm sorry, Nancy," she murmured. "I forgot that Oliver is your stepfather."

"Don't mind me," Nancy said quietly. She would have liked to add that she too would be glad to forget that Oliver Payne was her stepfather, but loyalty to her mother kept her silent.

They reached the entrance hall just as Mr. Baron was opening the door to admit visitors. A moment later a trickle of people began to flow into the museum. Most of them were children, usually accompanied by one or two adults. A group of boys climbed the stairs to the mineral room. A man stopped at the shop to inquire the way to the stegosaurus, which had been written up widely in the New England newspapers. Nancy's first day on her new job had begun.

Business was not rushed. Nancy watched and listened while Miss May waited on customers and answered questions about the various exhibits. Once she slipped away to make the tour of the downstairs halls by herself. Cousin Burton had disappeared from the Hall of Dinosaurs, but Professor Craig was standing near the unfinished mural, listening with a pleased expression to the awed comments of the people gathered around the stegosaurus. He gave Nancy several pointers on what he thought she should stress in the short talk she would soon be giving to visitors. Then he took her to the museum library, which was located in his office, and selected two books on prehistoric animals, urging her to take them home and read them carefully.

"Take notes on the animals that we have on exhibit here," he advised. "Sometimes people ask the most amazing questions, particularly the youngsters. If they stump you, I'm usually in my office and always happy to be of help. Never, never answer a question unless you're quite sure of the answer."

A worried frown clouded Nancy's face as she walked back to the shop. In taking this museum job, was she attempting more than she could handle? She lifted her chin. The answers to all those questions were in books and in the exhibits in the museum. She would read and read until she knew by heart the natural history of the animals and the conditions under which their bones had been found. And she would ask questions until Professor Craig and everyone else at the museum grew tired of answering her. She wasn't going to let this job defeat her!

Late in the afternoon, she made her first sale—to a woman and little boy who had just come down from the Indian room on the upper floor. Nancy took down several books on Indians to show to the eager, bright-eyed boy. After he had made his choice, she wrapped the book and put the money in the cash drawer with a warm feeling of achievement, not only because of her sale, but because she had helped the boy find a book that made him impatient to explore the pages inside its covers.

The last visitor had left. Professor Craig and Burton Payne had gone out together earlier, and the men from the taxidermist department and other basement rooms had followed. Miss May counted the money in the cash drawer and put it in a small metal box, which in turn was locked in a tiny vault in the thick wall.

"It's safe there until the end of the week," she told Nancy. "It would take an explosion to open this vault door. Not that anyone is likely to break into the museum—although we did have a robbery two weeks ago," she remembered.

"What was stolen?" Nancy asked with a chuckle. "A dinosaur bone?"

Mr. Baron, who was standing near, gave her an angry glance and muttered something under his breath as he started to climb the marble stairs to the second floor.

"Mr. Baron and Dan, the young man upstairs, are sensitive about the robbery," Miss May whispered. "But they can't be everywhere at once, and no one would dream of blaming them.

"What was taken wasn't of great value, so far as money values are concerned," she continued in a normal tone of voice, after Mr. Baron had made the turn in the stairs. "While Dan was showing visitors the Indian room, someone broke a case in the mineral room and stole three gem-cut peridots—semiprecious stones that are sometimes called cat's-eyes," she explained in answer to Nancy's questioning glance. "The odd thing about it was that a diamond, a ruby, and an emerald were in the same case, and the thief left them there in spite of their much greater value. So we figure that our thief is some sort of crank."

Mr. Baron was returning from his inspection of the upper rooms. Running ahead of him was a young man whom Miss May introduced to Nancy as Dan Stevens, the student geologist in charge of the mineral and Indian exhibits. He appeared to be in a great hurry, but he stopped to exchange cordial greetings. He was stocky in build and quite good looking, Nancy thought. He was well dressed, too, in a summer tweed jacket and tan slacks.

"Nice to have you working here, Nancy," he said. To Miss May he added, "I've got to step on it. Lucille is at a beauty shop downtown and I promised to pick her up and drive her home. She blows her top if I keep her waiting a second. Be seeing you around, Nancy!"

He waved his hand and banged out through the door. A few moments later, as Miss May and Nancy were descending the portico steps and Mr. Baron was carefully locking the heavy door, a small red car roared out of the parking lot behind the museum and barely missed a collision with another car it careened from the driveway into Elm Street.

"Poor Dan," said Miss May. "His best girl, Lucille Foster, keeps him in such a ferment running after her and trying to please her that sometimes he scarcely seems to know what he's doing."

Nancy smiled uncertainly. A young man so much in love was beyond her experience. For some reason, her thoughts flew to Alan Shelby and unconsciously she shook her head. She was sure that Alan was not the type to let any girl get him in a dither.

Nancy walked the block to her bus stop with Professor Craig's two books under her arm. The bus was hot and crowded, and she had to stand up all the way to Orchard Road. She wondered hungrily what they would be having for dinner, and she looked forward with pleasure to telling her mother about her experiences at the museum.

When she left the bus and started up Orchard Road, her step was not quite so springy as it had been that morning. She was conscious of feeling tired, but it was as much from the exhilaration and excitement of a new job as from physical fatigue, and deep inside her there was a wonderful feeling of contentment. She had found a place for herself, she liked her job, and she had made her first step toward independence.

She was glad to reach the Payne drive with its border plantings of trees and shady laurel, but when she neared the house and saw her mother and Karen sitting together on the terrace, her good feeling ebbed a little. They looked so cool and comfortable in their pastel summer dresses—and so companionable. For a moment, Nancy had the dreary sensation of being an intruder. She frowned at Karen, wishing that just for once her stepsister wasn't with her mother so that she could talk with Mother alone, as they used to do. Then Karen saw her. "Here's Nancy!" she cried, waving a welcome.

Nancy walked around and up the terrace steps. She felt happier when she saw how her mother's face lighted up at the sight of her. She went to her and bent down to kiss her, and Mrs. Payne threw her arm around Nancy and hugged her.

"Well, dear, how did it go?"

"Just splendid, Mother. I love Miss May, and working in the museum is a dream."

Nancy sat down in one of the lawn chairs and kicked off her flats. On a table beside Mrs. Payne was an amethyst glass pitcher of lemonade, beaded with frost and tinkling with ice. She poured lemonade into a tall glass and handed it to Nancy. "Welcome home," she said with a smile.

Nancy took a thirsty sip of the deliciously cold drink

and lay back in her chair with a little sigh of pleasure.
"Oh. This is good!"

Between sips of tangy-sweet lemonade, she told her
mother and Karen about her first day on the new job.
She felt her mother's loving interest reach out to her,
and it made a glow of good feeling spread all through
her.

"I like being a working girl," she said, wriggling her
toes contentedly. "But it's nice to come home, too."

The expression of quiet satisfaction that crossed her
mother's face surprised Nancy at first; then she understood the reason for it. For the first time since coming
to Glendale Falls, she had said "home" as if she were
really glad to be there.

Karen was full of the plans that she and Mrs. Payne
had made for the birthday party on Friday night. They
were to have a hamburger and hot-dog roast at the grill
on the other end of the terrace. Mrs. Payne had promised baked beans, salad, plenty of Cokes, and ice cream
to go with the cake.

"Minnie Bell always bakes me a chocolate cake," Karen ran on. "Three layers and scads of yummy icing.
We'll bring the record player outside so we can dance
on the terrace. I'll ask Father to get some Japanese lanterns."

Nancy sighed to herself. She was not a good dancer—
in fact she had never danced except with other girls.

"I've invited Barry, Rosalie Slade, Tom Greenway,
and Johnny Devlin. That will make six. I'll ask Louise
Burns, if I can find another boy." Karen pouted wor-

riedly. "I hope Ruthie Webster won't tag along and bring that silly turtle."

Nancy grinned lazily. "Violet should make an interesting guest. I bet she's crazy about hot dogs."

Suddenly she found the idea of Karen's party delightful. It would be pleasant to meet some other young people and to have some fun. She'd dance with Violet if no one else asked her!

The sound of a car on the drive announced the arrival of the master of the house. Nancy slipped on her shoes and rose hastily from her chair.

"I'll freshen up a bit before dinner," she told her mother.

Carrying her books and followed by Karen, who was still talking about her party, she ran upstairs, glad to have avoided meeting Mr. Payne in the hall. She went into the pink-tiled bathroom to comb her hair and wash her face and hands. Then she slipped into a fresh blouse and a gathered cotton skirt that Aunt Kathy had made for her. She wished she might put on her cool madras shorts, but Mr. Payne would not permit Karen and her to wear shorts or jeans to the dinner table.

Karen turned over the pages of the books Nancy had left on her desk. She wrinkled her nose in distaste. "Are you really going to read all this deep stuff?"

"You bet. I've got to cram—it's part of my job." Nancy tucked in her blouse. "But I like it, really I do."

Karen flipped the book shut. "I believe you actually do enjoy this stuff and all those old bones at the museum, dry as dust . . ."

"Dinosaurs aren't just old bones," Nancy said. "And Smilodon may be Miss May's cat, but the real Smilodon the saber-tooth isn't just a restoration of a huge ferocious cat. They're pages in the history of the earth, and by knowing about them we can better understand the earth as it is today."

Karen shook her curly head. "You sound like Cousin Burton. Honestly, Nancy, aren't you interested at all in just having fun and knowing boys?"

"Of course I am," Nancy assured her hastily. She didn't want Karen to start thinking of her as some sort of nut. "I met a nice boy today. He boards with Miss May and works at the college."

Karen't eyes brightened. "Well! I'm glad you came down to earth long enough to notice he was there. Why don't you invite him to my birthday party?"

"Maybe I will." Nancy smiled pensively, finding that she liked the suggestion.

5

Dan—and Alan

Nancy was waiting on the porch of the museum when Miss May arrived the next day, having come a little early in the hope of meeting Alan Shelby, but no chugging lawn mower broke the sunny summer stillness. Miss May's young boarder must be working on some other part of the campus.

If she didn't see Alan today, would she have the courage to telephone him at Miss May's and invite him to the cookout? She had never in her life telephoned a boy, and if this one refused her invitation, she'd want to crawl into a hole somewhere to hide her humiliation. She set her lips nervously. She wasn't pretty and she was too tall. At home in Maine, Alan probably had lots of girls. Maybe she shouldn't ask him after all.

Miss May gave Nancy a cheery greeting as she climbed the portico steps. A few moments later, Dan Stevens' red car flashed up the drive. When Dan came sprinting across the grass from the parking lot, he was flushed and out of breath.

"It's too hot to tear around," Miss May remarked.

Dan pulled out a handkerchief to mop his perspiring face.

"Professor Craig warned me not to be late again," he said. "I had to run Lucille out to her girl friend's house. I'm going to pick her up again tonight and take her to dinner at the *Jolly Silversmith*."

"Pretty swanky places you take that girl of yours," Miss May said dryly.

"Lucille likes to go where there's dancing and where she'll meet her friends. I don't belong to her crowd—I'm lucky that she'll give me a second glance," Dan said humbly.

"Maybe Lucille thinks she's the lucky one," Nancy suggested to the likable young man.

Dan gave her a grateful glance. "Lucille is the prettiest girl in Glendale Falls. She can have her pick of the boys."

Mr. Baron arrived and let them into the museum. Dan took the marble stairs two at a time. He always seemed to be in a rush. In a low voice, Miss May told Nancy that Dan was working his way through college. He was the oldest of a large family of children and the family was in very modest circumstances, while Lucille Foster belonged to the well-to-do country-club crowd.

"She's distractingly pretty, but she's also demanding and conceited. Dan really deserves a nicer girl. Why don't you set your cap for him, Nancy?"

Nancy laughed. "Now what chance would I have against the glamorous Lucille?"

It was really Alan about whom Nancy was thinking. She considered asking Miss May if he was over at the house. Perhaps she could dash across and ask him to the party. Then she changed her mind. She didn't want Miss May to think she was running after her boarder.

There was a steady stream of visitors at the museum that afternoon, and Nancy soon found herself so busy that she forgot Alan Shelby. Two visiting groups, one a garden club and one a Sunday-school class, arrived at separate times and were shown through the lower rooms by Miss May. Nancy tagged along and scribbled notes on a little pad she held in the palm of her hand. Afterward, business at the shop was brisk. Nancy sold two boxed mineral collections and several books. Today she was beginning to feel that she was really earning her salary.

On his way out of the museum, Burton Payne stopped at the shop to chat.

"You've made a hit with our bachelor, Nancy," Miss May teased. "He seldom has time to stop by and talk with just poor old me."

Burton turned to give her a long, grave look. To Nancy's surprise, Miss May's cheeks turned pink.

"Annie, you know you can have as much of my time as you desire—or anything else of mine that you want," the man said brusquely. Then he turned on his heel and strode out of the museum.

Well—what goes on here? Nancy wondered.

Miss May was silent as she went about putting the shop in order and counting the cash. She had to begin the count over again, as if her thoughts were on other matters. Afterward, she checked the rows of books on the shelves.

"Could you come early tomorrow, so we can type some orders before lunch?" she asked Nancy. Nancy was delighted. She would see Alan at lunch, and if she had a chance to talk to him alone, perhaps she might invite him to the party after all.

That night, after a good deal of reading in her room, Nancy wrote the first draft of her talk for the museum. Karen and her father were watching a television program downstairs. When Nancy's mother came looking for her, Nancy seized the opportunity to read her the sketch.

"It sounds fine to me," her mother assured her. "And it will be even better when you give it on the spot."

She put her arm around Nancy's shoulders as she sat at her desk by the window, and her eyes went from Nancy's eager, uptilted face to the pile of books and papers on the desk.

"I'm proud that you want to do well at the museum. But now, won't you come and join the family for the rest of the evening?"

Nancy switched off the lamp and stood up. "I guess I've soaked up all the natural history I can take at one sitting," she admitted.

In the living room, the television program was over and the color set was turned off.

"I'm ice-cream hungry," Mr. Payne greeted his wife and Nancy. "What say we raid the freezer?"

Nancy and Karen trailed their parents to the kitchen.

"Minnie Bell went to the movies with the Fosters' maid, their third this year," Karen told Nancy. "The last one told Minnie that she quit because Lucille and her mother expected her to be a personal maid, as well as cook, laundress, and what-not."

"Oh? I didn't know Lucille Foster lived near us," Nancy said, curious to know more about Dan Stevens' girl.

"They've lived up the road for about a year. Lucille goes to a private school. She's older than we. Do you know her?" Karen asked in surprise.

They sat down at the table in the breakfast area of the big modern kitchen. Mrs. Payne was taking cartons of ice cream out of the freezer. Mr. Payne was poking into jars and lifting the cover of the cake server in search of whatever Minnie might have tucked away.

"There's a fellow at the museum who's crazy about Lucille Foster," Nancy confided in a low voice.

"Oh, Nancy! Not the boy you were going to ask to my party?" Karen asked regretfully.

"No, not Alan. Lucille's beau is Dan Stevens, and he doesn't know there's another girl in the world."

At the counter, Mrs. Payne was taking the tops off cartons. "What will it be, girls?" she called gaily. "Cherry? Vanilla? Chocolate?"

"Mmm. Chocolate for me," Nancy said.

Karen and her father chose cherry. Nancy carried the heaped-up saucers of ice cream to the table, while Karen fetched spoons from the silver drawer, and Mr. Payne produced half a sponge cake and a plate of cookies from Minnie Bell's stores.

They made a cozy-looking family group as they sat around the table, but Nancy sighed to herself when Mr. Payne began to question her about how the Big Black exhibit was progressing.

Because of an extremely busy day at the plant, Mr. Payne had been late for dinner and Nancy had been spared his usual questioning about the doings at the museum. Now he began to complain angrily about his brother-in-law's dilatory methods in getting his bear mounted. Reminding herself that she was trying to like him for her mother's sake, Nancy answered him patiently, almost as if she were trying to humor a child who might go into a tantrum if he didn't get his own way. If she had been watching her mother, she would have realized that this attitude toward her stepfather was distressing her more than if Nancy's answers had been short and impatient.

"They've started to put in the background, and it's beautiful. Professor Craig says positively that the bear will be on display by Saturday."

"It had better be!" her stepfather said explosively. "I'll be in on Saturday to check on it. I would have been there to light a fire under John Craig before now if it hadn't been for this deluge of visiting directors and stockholders at the plant."

He cut himself a piece of Minnie's orange sponge cake and then smiled at all of them in a sudden change of mood.

"Don't forget that the midsummer banquet is the week after next! I hope you've bought yourself something gorgeous to wear, Amy. I don't want anyone to outshine my wife."

Mrs. Payne gave him a bright smile. "Just wait until you see my gown—and get the bill for it!"

"Dreamy ivory lace," Karen put in. "Really delicious."

"Good!" pronounced Mr. Payne. "It sounds like just the thing to show off Grandmother's topaz necklace."

When Alan Shelby returned to the May house for lunch the next day, Nancy was typing book orders in the little den at the end of the hall. Smilodon was crouched on the desk, watching the play of the typewriter keys and sometimes batting at them with his paw.

"I see you have a helper," Alan said from the doorway. Smilodon jumped down and padded over to rub against him. "How's the job going, Nancy?" Alan stooped to scratch the cat's golden head, then straightened his tall figure to lounge against the wall.

"Never a dull moment," she replied, stopping work to smile at him. It was a wonder to her how much at home she felt with this boy. This was only the third time she had seen him, yet she felt as if they were old friends. "How is the grass-mowing, shrub-pruning department doing?"

"Keeps me hopping," Alan admitted. "I could stand some recreation at night. I'm helping the carpenter make some repairs on a greenhouse belonging to the botany department," he explained. "It's got to be finished today and I may have to work overtime to do it, but how about seeing a movie with me tomorrow night? The budget might even stretch to a hamburger and soda."

The unexpected invitation sent a glow of pleasure over Nancy. Then she sighed. Her first invitation for a date in Glendale Falls and she had to refuse!

She stood up and crossed the room. Tall as she was, she had to look up at Alan. Her green eyes were shadowed with regret.

"I'd love to go to the movies with you, but I can't go tomorrow." Please, please ask me sometime again, she was saying silently. "Actually, I was going to invite you to come to my stepsister's party tomorrow night. It's a cookout. I thought you could go home with me when the museum closes."

She drew a happy little breath. She had so dreaded asking Alan to the party, but the invitation had come out easily, after all, and she could tell by Alan's smile that he was pleased.

"I'll drive you home in my old station wagon," Alan said. "It's mighty nice of you and your stepsister to want me."

"It's really selfishness on my part," Nancy confessed. "You see, I'm new in Glendale Falls, too, and I don't know any of Karen's friends. I'd like a friend of my own to back me up when I meet her gang tomorrow night."

"You've got him!" Alan said, grinning at her.

How nice he was! It almost seemed a miracle to Nancy that, plain as she was, this boy liked her.

"Lunch in five minutes!" Miss May called from the kitchen.

Alan took the stairs two at a time to tidy himself before appearing at the table. Nancy hummed to herself as she pulled the last book order from the typewriter and put the cover on the machine. She did not feel romantic about Alan, as some of the girls at school had felt about boys, but it was delightful to have him for a friend.

At the shop in the afternoon, Nancy remembered that she had not bought a birthday gift for Karen. She looked over the jewelry in the case and chose a yellow enameled butterfly pin.

At the breakfast table the next morning, Karen was enchanted when she opened the little box containing Nancy's gift. She immediately pinned the sunny butterfly to her blue denim blouse. Her stepmother had given her a little French beaded clutch bag, and her father's gift was a string of cultured pearls, but she seemed to like Nancy's butterfly pin fully as much as the more expensive gifts.

"Be sure to get home as soon as you can tonight," she urged Nancy, following her to the door when she was ready to leave for the museum after lunch. "My, you look nice today!" she added, watching Nancy go down the steps to the drive.

The compliment pleased Nancy, and she turned and made her stepsister a little curtsy. Last night she had washed and set her short hair and now the sun shimmered on the loose dark waves. She would not have time to change her dress when she returned with Alan that night, so she was dressed for the party in a rose colored denim skirt and a green-and-rose striped blouse with a demure round collar. The material was supposed to stay fresh and unwrinkled all day. It was with a pleasant feeling of looking her best that Nancy started down Orchard Road to the bus stop.

She had almost reached the highway when a sharp blast on an auto horn made her leap aside as a car came tearing around a curve behind her. Her heart pounding at her near escape, she crowded herself back against the bushes at the side of the road. The small red convertible rushed past her at crazy speed and careened onto the highway on two wheels. Then there was a shriek of rubber as the car slammed to a stop.

Nancy stepped back into the road and started to walk to the bus stop on the corner. The red car went into reverse and shot back toward her. It came to a shuddering stop with another loud shriek of rubber. Nancy was scarcely surprised to see that the driver was Dan Stevens. There couldn't be two such awful drivers in small red convertibles!

"You all but mowed me down!" she chided Dan.

Beside Dan sat a stunning blond girl in white shorts and blouse, a scarlet sweater slung around her shoulders and a tennis racket on her knees. She regarded Nancy with cold blue eyes and nodded only slightly when Dan introduced them. Nancy had already guessed that she was Lucille Foster.

Dan looked harried, as usual. "I didn't recognize you at first, Nancy," he said. "I'm taking Lucille out to the country club. Squeeze in with us and I'll give you a lift to the museum."

Dan's car was tiny and the beautiful blonde looked

anything but welcoming. Nancy smiled and shook her head.

"Thanks, Dan, but my bus is about due. I'd better take it—I don't want to be late."

Dan groaned as if her words reminded him of his many transgressions along that line.

"Step on it, Dan," Lucille snapped, "or I'm the one who'll be late for my date with Doris."

Dan waved his hand to Nancy, and the car shot ahead. With a feeling of relief, Nancy signaled the bus, which was just coming around the curve. Dan was such a terrible driver that she would have preferred hiking to the museum to riding in his tortured car.

Half a mile down the highway, near the place where the country club road turned off, the bus passed a small red convertible stalled by the side of the road. Lucille was standing beside it, looking perfectly furious. A scarlet-faced Dan was rolling a spare tire toward the front of the car.

Oh, poor Dan! Nancy thought. Lucille was going to be late for her date after all.

Miss May frowned worriedly when Nancy told her that Dan was probably going to be late again.

"That girl is going to lose Dan his job! Professor Craig has warned him time and again. Nancy, do you think you could take over upstairs until Dan gets here? Perhaps, if he isn't too late, we can cover up for him."

"I can try." Like Miss May and Mr. Baron, Nancy didn't want to see Dan lose his job because of his heedless devotion to the selfish Lucille.

During her few days at the museum, Nancy had not yet found the time to visit the upstairs rooms. Now she followed Mr. Baron up the marble stairs, which turned on a broad landing and then ascended to the top floor. In the upper hall, light came through the tall windows that stretched from the portico to the roof. A desk and a chair stood before the windows. Two doors opened off the hall, one leading into the mineral room and the other to the Indian exhibits.

"Just sit here at the desk," Mr. Baron told Nancy. "If the museum opens before Dan gets here, you'll have to make the round of the rooms from time to time. If anyone asks questions, tell them the regular attendant will be along soon—and let's hope that he will be."

Mr. Baron hurried back downstairs, grumbling, to take over the shop while Miss May conducted an early group of visitors through the lower halls.

Nancy sat down at Dan's desk. The upper floor seemed vast and silent, and she thought uneasily about the robbery that had taken place up here. She got up and walked to the door of the mineral room, not liking the idea of being alone to guard the valuable jewels and gold nuggets in the show cases.

Scattered here and there on the floor of the big room were huge specimens of mineral-bearing rocks. Nancy bent to read the tags on some of them—petrified wood, marble, anthracite. She turned to the glass cases and found the displays more interesting. There were gold nuggets, nodules of silver, and pieces of quartz veined with gold. Another case contained rough chunks of amethyst, rose quartz, rock crystal, and aquamarine.

She was admiring some jade in a third case when she sensed that someone was standing behind her. She whirled around, then gave a gasp of relief.

"Dan Stevens! You frightened me, coming in so silently."

He chuckled. "If I had been that robber, I could have bashed you over the head with a chunk of quartz."

"I don't think that's funny. And you'd better watch out! They say criminals always return to the scene of the crime."

"The fellow won't be back," Dan said confidently. "And he wasn't a criminal—only some kind of crank. He could have scooped up a handful of precious stones along with the three peridots he did take, but he didn't touch any of the really valuable stones. He probably did it just for kicks."

"Well, he's a thief just the same," Nancy insisted.

Dan took her arm and steered her over to a long case placed directly below some of the tiny high windows of this upper hall. With a murmur of pleasure, Nancy bent to get a closer view of the beautifully cut jewels displayed on bits of black velvet: sparkling blue-white diamonds, glowing deep-green emeralds, dark-blue sapphires, and dazzling golden topazes. Dan chuckled at her rapt expression.

"These stones always make the girls' eyes bug out," he said. "Lucille almost went crazy when she came up here. She loves jewelry." He pointed out the row of semiprecious stones ranged a step below the precious gems. There were beryls, amethysts, garnets, and citrine quartz.

"They're almost as lovely as the others," Nancy breathed.

The piece of velvet on the shelf below the precious emeralds was empty. The card in front of it read: Peridot. Evening emerald. Cat's-eye.

"The thief broke the glass and grabbed the three peridots that were on that velvet," said Dan. "They're worth about fifty dollars. The precious emerald is worth a thousand. Yet he took the peridots and left the emerald, not to mention the diamond and the ruby and other precious gems. So I guess we could say that he was really easy on the museum."

"He would have done better to let the stones alone entirely," Nancy reminded him tartly.

Voices and the sound of people on the stairs warned them that the museum had opened.

"I'm glad you made it on time," Nancy told Dan.

"So am I, sister. I had to go some."

I bet you did, thought Nancy.

"I saw your car beside the road," she said aloud. "It's a shame you had to have a flat."

"Yeah. Lucille was furious—and scared. We almost swerved into a pole. She's been nagging me about getting new tires." The familiar harried expression crossed Dan's face. "I can't save money for tires or a new car and still take her around to the expensive places where she wants to eat and dance." He smiled wryly. "I shouldn't be griping to you about my troubles, but you're a comfortable girl to talk to. And a doll for taking over for me up here."

"I was glad to do it, Dan."

Nancy thought it was a shame that someone like Lucille had to get her claws into a nice fellow like Dan!

After the museum closed that afternoon, Nancy walked home with Miss May to wait for Alan. He looked hot and grimy when he dashed into the house from some distant part of the campus, but he soon appeared again, his dark hair slicked back neatly after his shower, and his jeans and work shirt changed for a white shirt and a pair of gray slacks.

"I'll get my car from the parking lot," he told Nancy.

Alan's station wagon was a vintage model, but it showed signs of loving care. He had given it a skillful paint job, and it had a well-polished look. It started so smoothly that it was evident that he took equally good care of the motor, and to Nancy's delight, after days of watching Dan Stevens' crazy driving, Alan proved to be a driver who kept his car under control every minute. As they drove toward the suburbs, he apologized for not going faster.

"An old wagon like this, you can't push her too hard."

"This is just fine," Nancy said softly, meaning every word.

Alan told Nancy how lucky he felt to be boarding with Miss May.

"She makes me feel more as if I belonged than I do at home. You see," he explained, "my mother is dead. Dad married again and there are four younger children, so our house is pretty crowded."

"It seems strange," Nancy said, "that you should have a stepmother and I a stepfather, and we're both strangers in Glendale Falls."

"Gives us something more in common. How do you get along with your new pa?"

"Well," Nancy said slowly, "I just can't think of him as my father. He means to be kind, but . . ."

Alan gave an understanding nod. "I know. My stepmother doesn't mean to be cranky, but with her own younger kids, she could do without a strapping stepson cluttering the house. And she has no patience with my plans for going to college. Of course I'll have to earn my own way, because she's talked Dad into believing that it would be better for me to go right to work in the lumber mill when I graduate from high school next year." His strong jaw tightened. "I've worked at my uncle's fishing and hunting camp during vacations ever since I was old enough to split kindling and paddle a canoe, and I've saved almost a thousand dollars toward my college fund."

"That's wonderful," Nancy said. "Are you planning to go to Glendale College?"

He shook his head. "I guess not. I imagine I won't be very popular around Glendale." While Nancy was puzzling over that remark, Alan gave her a sidelong grin.

"I should be telling you how pretty you look in that outfit, instead of grousing away about my troubles. But you're an easy person to talk to, Nancy."

Well! thought Nancy. The second compliment and from the second boy that day!

"I'm just not the type that provokes gallant sayings," she said. "No glamour! The sister type."

"You have plenty of glamour in my eyes, Green Eyes," Alan said quickly. "Plus something a lot more attractive. You make a fellow feel as if you're genuinely interested in being friends. Most girls just latch on for dates."

"Now don't be so hard on girls," Nancy protested.

"I guess I really don't know much about girls," Alan admitted. "I haven't had the time for steady dating." Nancy's heart gave a happy little skip at the discovery that there was no steady girl in Maine after all.

Suddenly she realized that they had almost reached Orchard Road. "Take the next road on the left," she told Alan.

"I didn't realize that I was coming to such a swanky neighborhood," Alan said, as they drove up Orchard Road and turned into the Payne driveway.

Two strange cars were parked near the house. Alan parked his station wagon behind a racy yellow sports car and helped Nancy out.

A mouth-watering aroma of broiling bacon and hamburgers hung on the air, and the sound of young voices and laughter came from the terrace, where there was a cluster of young people around the brick fireplace and grill. Nearby, a redwood picnic table was set with bowls of salad, a big brown pot of bubbling baked beans, and other good things to eat.

Nancy and Alan mounted the terrace steps and started to join the crowd, but just then Mrs. Payne stepped through one of the living-room windows.

"I've been waiting to welcome your friend, Nancy." She turned to Alan with a pleasant smile.

"Mother, this is Alan Shelby," said Nancy. "Alan, my mother, Mrs. Payne."

Mrs. Payne held out her hand. "I'm delighted to meet you, Alan."

Alan just stood there with a dazed expression on his lean face. He looked from Mrs. Payne to Nancy.

"Did you say Payne?" he demanded. "*Payne?*"

"Yes, of course."

"Nancy, is your stepfather *Oliver* Payne?"

Mrs. Payne let her hand fall. "What is it, Alan? What's troubling you?"

At that moment Mr. Payne followed his wife out of the house. Seeing Alan, he stopped short.

"Alan Shelby!" he boomed. "How do you happen to be in Glendale Falls? I'm delighted that you've come to see me." He strode across the terrace with his hand outstretched.

While Nancy and her mother watched in amazement, Alan's face hardened to a mask of hate. His eyes blazed and his lips curled back in something that looked like a snarl. He ignored Oliver Payne's outstretched hand.

"I didn't come to see you!" He fairly spat the words out. "If I had known that this was your house, wild horses couldn't have dragged me within a mile of it."

Without a glance at Nancy, he strode down the terrace steps and back to where he had parked his station wagon.

"Alan!" Mr. Payne shouted after him. He stood at the top of the steps frowning at the unheeding boy.

By now Karen had noticed the late arrivals and she came running over to where Nancy stood clinging to her mother's arm.

"Was that your date, Nancy?" she cried. "Where's he going?"

"He just drove Nancy home, dear," Mrs. Payne said quickly. "He couldn't stay for the party." Her hand closed over Nancy's. Nancy was still trembling from the incredible scene she had witnessed between her new friend and her stepfather.

Sensing that something was wrong, Karen glanced inquiringly from Nancy and her mother to her father's outraged face. Finally she said, "It's too bad your date couldn't stay, Nancy. But come on and join the crowd."

Nancy gulped. "I'll be right over."

Karen returned to her friends, glancing back once over her shoulder.

Standing as if they had been rooted to the spot, Nancy, her mother, and Mr. Payne listened to the sound of Alan's car going down the drive.

6

The story of Big Black

"Why, that young idiot has actually gone away," Mr. Payne blustered, when the sound of the car died in the distance. "How did he happen to come here? Did you bring him, Nancy?"

She held her head high. "Yes. I invited him to Karen's party. He's working in maintenance at the college and boarding with Miss May."

Mr. Payne looked amazed at this bit of information. "I doubt that it was just a summer job that brought Alan to Glendale," he said thoughtfully.

"What is all this about?" asked Mrs. Payne. "The boy comes from Maine. Nancy thought he was a stranger in town."

"It was in Maine that I met him. He was working as a fishing guide at his uncle's sportsmen's camp. That was last summer . . ."

"When you shot Big Black?" Nancy asked slowly.

Oliver Payne gave her a keen look from under his

heavy brows. "Has Alan said anything to you about Big Black?"

"No. He's never mentioned the bear. He didn't know that you're my stepfather."

Nancy bit her lip, mulling the puzzle over in her mind. Did the black bear her stepfather had shot in Maine last summer have something to do with the reason why the name of Payne, and the mere appearance of her stepfather, had sent Alan into a state of fury?

Mr. Payne's next words confirmed her suspicion. "Alan went almost out of his mind when I shot that bear. When my guide, his own cousin, and I brought Black back to camp, we thought for a while that the crazy young fool was going to shoot *us*. His uncle had to send him home until I had left the camp. Afterward I heard that he came back and gave his cousin a severe beating."

"But, Oliver, why should the boy make such a fuss about your shooting a bear?" Mrs. Payne asked. "After all, his uncle was running a sportsmen's camp."

"Oh, he told some tall story about the bear having been a pet that he had raised from a cub."

Light dawned on Nancy. "Big Black was Alan's *pet?*"

"The bear was running wild in the woods—and when you see him mounted, you'll realize how huge he was. The boy was lying."

The words did not convince Nancy. Her heart ached with sympathy for Alan.

"Now I wonder what brought him to Glendale College," Mr. Payne was saying. "I'll go over and have a talk with him tomorrow."

"He needed a job to help with his college fund," Nancy said.

"He could have a more congenial and better-paying job working at his uncle's camp. I'm going to make sure he didn't come down here to take a pot shot at me some dark night."

"Oliver!" Mrs. Payne cried in a shocked voice. "Do you think you're in danger?"

"Alan's not the kind to shoot any one down," Nancy protested. "Of course he was upset if you shot his bear."

"He was more than upset—he was crazy mad."

"Perhaps you should have him questioned by the authorities," Mrs. Payne said worriedly.

"I'll talk to him first," her husband decided.

"Nancy, come on!" Karen called impatiently from the other end of the terrace, where her guests were finding seats at the table.

For the rest of the evening, Nancy made herself agreeable to Karen's guests, friendly young people who welcomed her to their neighborhood crowd. She toasted frankfurters, served beans, and passed bottles of cold Coke. She joined in the cheer when Minnie Bell carried out the three-layer chocolate cake with its fifteen pink candles and garlands of sugar roses. Through it all her thoughts were with Alan Shelby.

Not for a moment did she believe that Alan meant any harm to Mr. Payne. She longed to hear Alan's side of the story of Big Black. And she wondered with a heavy heart if the fact that Mr. Payne was her step-father would make any difference in Alan's feelings toward her.

At twilight, the Payne handyman lighted the Japanese lanterns that had been strung on the terrace, and the young people danced to the music of Karen's favorite records. Nancy was an extra girl, but the other girls cheerfully took turns sitting out while she danced with their dates. In spite of her doubts about her dancing, Nancy happily breezed through one dance after another, and her confidence grew with every number.

"I expected Ruthie to show up here tonight with Violet," she said during her dance with Barry Webster.

He grinned. "Ruthie is spending a week with her best friend, and I'm riding herd on that pesky turtle while she's away."

"I wonder if Ruthie's ever seen the prehistoric turtle at the Payne Museum. I'd love to show it to her."

"I don't think she's ever been to the museum. She was sick when her class at school visited it last spring."

Nancy laughed gaily. "Then I'll have the fun of showing her Archelon."

On Saturday morning, Mr. Payne asked Nancy what time she was leaving for the museum. "I'll drive you over. I want to speak to that boy."

Nancy hesitated. The sight of her driving up with Mr. Payne in his sleek Cadillac might really put the finishing touch on her friendship with Alan. But how could she get out of riding with her stepfather without being rude? And besides, he *was* her stepfather, and if Alan wanted to be friends, he would just have to accept that fact, just as she herself must accept it.

"I'm going a little early today," she replied.

"That's all right," Mr. Payne said. "I'll take you."

She felt the need to discuss this matter of Alan and Mr. Payne with Miss May, who, she felt, wouldn't be so prejudiced as her mother. After the party Friday night, Mrs. Payne had gone to Nancy's room to talk about Alan's queer behavior.

"If Alan Shelby is the kind of boy who would threaten people with a rifle, I don't want you to have anything to do with him, Nancy."

"But, Mother, probably Alan just waved his rifle, and Mr. Payne thought he was being threatened," Nancy protested. "Alan doesn't seem like a violent boy. There's something we don't understand about this . . ."

"Until we do understand, we must take your father's word that the boy is wild," her mother replied firmly.

"You needn't worry about me being friends with Alan." There was a note of bitterness in Nancy's voice. "Now that he knows I'm Oliver Payne's stepdaughter, I'm probably poison to him anyhow."

"Well, dear, you'll meet lots of attractive boys when you start school next fall. So don't be downhearted about Alan Shelby."

But Nancy couldn't help being downhearted. She was sure that she would never meet another boy she'd like as much as she liked Alan.

Shortly before noon Mr. Payne parked his car in front of the May house and followed Nancy up the walk. Nancy gave the knocker a faint thud, hoping with all her heart that no one would answer it, but after a moment Alan opened the door. His face darkened when he saw Mr. Payne.

"Alan, I want to talk to you," Mr. Payne said over Nancy's shoulder.

Alan's eyes narrowed to glittering slits. "Look, Mr. Payne," he rapped out, "I made it plain last night that we have nothing to talk about. Maybe you can get me fired from the college force, since I understand you're a big man in this town, but you can't bully me into condoning what you did last summer in Maine. You—you murderer!"

Nancy gasped. Her stepfather's face flushed beet-red.

"Alan," he said sharply, "that's a childish way to look at the matter . . ."

In his determination to talk to Alan, he pushed Nancy ahead of him into the house. Alan had already turned his back and was striding down the hall. Nancy was crowded against the wall as her stepfather brushed by her.

"Alan!" His voice was an angry shout.

They heard the back door slam, and then Miss May was facing Mr. Payne from the kitchen doorway.

"Alan has gone. I should think it would be plain that he wants no part of you, Oliver," she said coldly.

"Do you think I'm going to allow that young whelp to go about Glendale Falls branding me as a murderer? Why can't he calm down and listen to my explanation of why I shot that bear?"

"From Alan's point of view, there's no explanation. In

his eyes, you murdered his pet bear while the poor beast was peacefully feeding in a berry patch, where he'd been taught that he'd be safe from hunters. Alan told me the disgraceful story last night." Miss May's eyes were sharp with scorn.

Mr. Payne fairly shook with indignation. "Annie, I know you're prejudiced against me . . ."

"And with good cause," she broke in.

"But even you cannot believe that I am so low as to shoot a pet animal for sport! All I knew was that Black was a giant among black bears, and I needed a bear to complete the exhibits in the Wildlife Hall at the Museum. It was Alan himself who told me, at the fireside one night, about this king among bears who roamed the slopes of a mountain near his uncle's camp. And it was Alan's cousin who guided me to the berry patch . . ."

"After you had bribed him with a hundred dollars, and after you had asked Alan to guide you and he had refused."

"Annie, listen to me!" Mr. Payne glanced from her to Nancy as if he were begging them to try to understand his side of the matter. "Big Black had reached his prime. In a year or two he would have started to grow old. Wasn't it better for him to be in the museum at the peak of his glory than to go downhill to a miserable old age in the woods, while his eyes grew dim, his coat thin and dull . . ."

Nancy was surprised to hear her own voice. "Maybe Big Black would have preferred to grow old as nature intended. Maybe he loved life as much as we do. After

all, for a bear the conditions you speak of are normal . . ."

"I'm not going to discuss a bear's feelings with you,
Nancy," her stepfather said impatiently. "It's Alan Shelby's irresponsible accusation that I am concerned
about. How am I going to look before Hank Rawlings
and the Museum Associates if word gets about that I
shot a tame bear?"

There was no sympathy in the two pairs of eyes that
were regarding him.

"If you knew, or even guessed, that the bear was a
pet, you'd deserve all the ridicule and disgust that
you'd get." The glance Miss May gave him cut like a
knife.

Why, thought Nancy. Here's another one! Miss May,
Alan, Cousin Burton—all with a feeling of keen hostility toward Oliver Payne! A feeling of dismay and un-
easiness grew inside her.

"I didn't know Black was a pet!" The little hall re-
sounded with Mr. Payne's angry voice. "I don't believe it even now. If you could have seen the brute
about to charge me . . ."

"He probably sensed that he was in danger," said
Nancy.

"Nancy," demanded her stepfather, "whose side are
you on?"

Miss May came to Nancy's help. "You must have
been aware, Oliver, that other hunters had spared this
famous bear."

"It was a silly taboo. Someone was bound to shoot

him sometime—and I needed him for my group in the museum."

"There you have summed it up nicely," Miss May told him in a cold, unfriendly voice. "You wanted the bear and you shot it."

He made an angry sound and strode to the door. There he turned to look back at Nancy. For a moment she feared that he was going to order her to go home with him. She lifted her chin and met his eyes bravely. Her stepfather cleared his throat, then said in a milder tone, "Nancy, tell that boy that I insist upon talking to him. He's to telephone me at home or at the office."

He went out, closing the door with what Nancy felt was great restraint.

"Do you suppose he'll get Alan fired?" she asked worriedly.

"No," Miss May said. "Oliver is quick-tempered and domineering, but he's not mean. He feels humiliated because of Alan's charge that he shot a tame animal, and he'll try to silence Alan or make him retract his words. It could be, too, that for once his conscience is troubling him, and that's the reason for all the bluster." She gave Nancy a rueful glance. "Dear me, I keep forgetting that Oliver is your stepfather."

"There are lots of times when I'd like to forget it too," Nancy said. Then her cheeks reddened as the now familiar feeling of disloyalty to her mother came over her. "I shouldn't have said that," she murmured unhappily. "Mr. Payne is awfully kind to me. But I—I like Alan and I can't help but feel that there's some truth in his story."

Miss May linked her arm through Nancy's and walked with her to the kitchen.

"I'll tell you the whole story of Big Black, just as Alan told it to me last night." She glanced at the clock. "We have time for a cup of coffee before the museum opens."

She poured two cups of coffee and set a plate of Danish pastry on the table. Then she began the story.

"It was six years ago, in June, that Alan found a tiny lost bear cub wandering along a road near the mill town where he lives. He took the cub home and cared for him. Later he heard of a female bear who had been shot by a farmer while she was making off with one of his pigs. This must have been the cub's mother, for the farm was on the road where Alan had found the little one."

Miss May stirred cream into her coffee. Nancy pinched off a piece of buttery pastry and waited eagerly for the rest of the story.

"Alan took the cub with him when he went to his uncle's camp for the summer. By that time he and the bear had become great friends. The cub had the run of the camp, and his cuteness and rollicking play endeared him to the visiting sportsmen. Everyone petted and spoiled him. In the autumn, Alan took Blackie home with him, and when cold weather set in, the cub went into hibernation in a cave Alan had dug under a shed and lined with leaves.

"When Blackie appeared again in the spring, he had grown considerably. He was bubbling with mischief and hungry all the time. Alan's stepmother wasn't happy about having him about the place, and except for the times when they went for rambles in the woods, Alan had to keep him chained up."

"Poor wild creature," Nancy murmured.

Miss May nodded. "That's the way Alan felt about Blackie. Now that the cub was growing up, he couldn't be happy in captivity. And furthermore, Alan didn't have a permit to keep a wild animal captive. Blackie was old enough now to fend for himself, and so Alan decided that he must go back to the wilds.

"When they returned to the camp that summer, Alan began taking the cub for long walks. Then he would steal away and leave Blackie by himself. Blackie always found his way back, but he spent longer and longer periods by himself in the woods. And then some gun-happy, so-called sportsman took a shot at the big, glossy cub and grazed him with a bullet. Blackie took off into the woods and Alan didn't see him again before the camp closed. He thought he had lost him forever."

"But they did meet again? Of course, they must have!" Nancy said, bright-eyed with interest.

"Yes, they met again the next summer. Blackie never returned to the camp, but he must have been on the lookout for his friend. One day, when Alan was fishing alone along a mountain stream, a huge black bear came out of the woods. Alan's heart was in his throat before a friendly 'Woof' told him that the bear was Blackie— Big Black now, the biggest, handsomest bear Alan had ever seen.

"Big Black had become wild enough, though, so that he wouldn't go close enough for Alan to pet him," Miss May continued, after a sip of coffee. "But Alan had no desire to become unduly familiar with the huge animal. Alan tells me that bears are intelligent, but also unpredictable, and they themselves are scarcely aware of their own tremendous strength. One playful sweep of Big Black's paw could have ripped off Alan's arm or scalped him.

"The bear stayed fairly close to Alan all the time he was fishing, and every so often Alan would toss him a trout, which he ate with pleasure. Later, he ambled after Alan part of the way home, but disappeared before the camp came into view."

"That bullet wound had taught him that bears can't trust men," Nancy remarked sadly.

Miss May nodded. "But his old love and trust of Alan remained, and he always appeared to join him on lone fishing trips and hikes. And often, when Alan was guiding one of his uncle's guests, he would sense Big Black's nearness, even though the bear stayed out of sight."

"How wonderful it would be to have a friendship like that with a wild animal," Nancy said a little enviously. Her conviction that Alan was a remarkable boy grew stronger.

Miss May continued: "As the years passed, Big Black became famous, for in spite of his shyness, people caught glimpses of him from time to time. He was the king of the woods, and the slopes of a rocky mountain near the camp were his special domain. Alan told the story of the orphan cub to all the sportsmen who came to the camp and asked them not to harm him. They all respected Alan's wishes, and the bear kept his part of the truce by never raiding the food supplies at the camp or the livestock of farmers, as some of his less cautious relatives were wont to do. He had become a legend by the time Oliver Payne went to stay at the camp. Unfortunately, Oliver was looking for a fine specimen for a habitat group at the museum . . ."

"So he shot Big Black! Oh!" Nancy cried bitterly, "I don't blame Alan for hating him!"

"Nancy," Annie May said seriously, "there was a time when I used to hate Oliver Payne for wrecking my dreams and ruining my life. Years ago I was engaged to Burton Payne."

Nancy's eyes widened.

"At that time Oliver was obsessed with the idea that Burton should marry a girl—a distant relative—who owned the majority of stock in the Payne Krispys Company. The two cousins had been brought up by their grandmother and she was considered the head of the family. Oliver convinced his grandmother that I was not the girl for Burton, and she set herself against our marriage. Oliver then came to me and accused me of ruining Burton's life. I was appalled at having been the cause of so much trouble in their family. I ran away and took a position as librarian in a Midwestern town. No one but my parents knew where I had gone and they kept my secret. Burton thought that I had run away from him.

"I didn't return to Glendale Falls until just a few years ago, when my mother was in poor health and needed me. Then when Mother died, I stayed on and opened the shop in the museum."

"And neither you nor Cousin Burton ever fell in love with anyone else?" Nancy's eyes had filled with tears.

Miss May shook her head sadly. "For me no one could ever take Burton's place."

"I think he's still in love with you." Nancy burst out. "Why don't you marry him now?"

Miss May gave a tremulous little laugh. "We're middle-aged now and set in our ways. It's better to keep the memory of our youthful, romantic love."

"What happened to the rich girl Mr. Payne wanted Burton to marry?" Nancy wondered.

"After a while, Oliver persuaded her to marry *him*. She was Karen's mother."

Nancy thought this over. "There certainly are a lot of people with good cause to hate Mr. Payne."

"I hated him bitterly for a long time," Miss May admitted. "Then I came to realize that the one I was really hurting with my hatred was myself. Hatred is a deadly poison that can destroy the person who harbors it. I feel so much more clean and free since I stopped hating. I mean to have a talk about this with Alan."

"Miss May," Nancy said anxiously, "do you believe that Alan came to Glendale Falls to take some kind of vengeance on Mr. Payne?"

"No, I do *not!* He probably was drawn here by a desire to see his bear again, even if it's mounted and in a glass case."

"I can't see how that would be any comfort to him," Nancy said with a deep sigh.

7

A party that wasn't fun

When Miss May and Nancy went over to the museum, they met Professor Craig in the entrance hall.

"Well, Nancy," he greeted her, "you can tell your step-father that Big Black is in his display case and he looks magnificent."

It wasn't quite time for the shop to open so Nancy hurried along the corridor to the Hall of Wildlife. She stopped short when she saw Alan Shelby and Burton Payne sitting on a bench in front of Big Black's lighted case. Alan was talking, and from the way his words poured out and the emotion on his face, Nancy guessed that he was telling the story of Big Black. She approached slowly, not certain how Alan would greet her.

"Son, you have my sympathy," Burton was saying as Nancy came up. "I've had shattering first-hand experience with Oliver's juggernaut tactics."

"I don't know why I've bothered you with my story —a perfect stranger . . ." Alan said wonderingly.

"When I saw you hunched over on this bench, I felt

that you were in deep trouble. I sat down beside you because I wanted to help if I could." Burton smiled. "Sometimes two strangers meet and realize at once that they were meant to be friends. I work here at the museum. My name is Payne—Burton Payne."

"Payne!" Alan jumped to his feet.

"I hope you won't let my name stand in the way of our being friends," Burton said quickly.

At that moment Alan became aware of Nancy's presence. His face hardened and he swung on his heel and strode away without a word. Nancy's mouth trembled as she looked after him.

"I can't help it that my mother is married to Mr. Payne!" she called out.

"You know that young fellow?" Burton Payne asked in surprise.

"Yes. He boards with Miss May."

This bit of information surprised Burton still more. "Annie never took a boarder before. She must think young Shelby is all right."

Nancy nodded rather absently. She had swung around and found herself looking at the mounted figure of Big Black. A low cry escaped her. "He looks so real!"

The artist who had created the background, and the taxidermist, had done a magnificent job. The huge glossy-coated black bear seemed almost to be breathing as he stood among low bushes gemmed with clusters of silvery-blue berries. In the background a forest of pines and black spruce clustered beneath the rocky escarpment of a mountain boldly outlined against a turquoise-blue sky. Nancy drew a deep breath. Poor Alan! How it must have torn his heart to see his bear looking so alive against the familiar background!

That day even Dan Stevens was out of sorts. He didn't pause at the shop to chat when he entered the museum, but tramped heavily upstairs with a frown on his face. At closing time, he didn't rush away as usual, but bade Miss May and Nancy a glum "good night" and walked slowly toward the parking lot, like a man who was carrying a heavy burden.

"He must have had a quarrel with that girl of his," Miss May said. "And if you ask me, it's the best thing that could happen to him."

Later, as she was walking up Orchard Road, Nancy was passed by an expensive-looking white convertible with a handsome young man at the wheel. Lucille was sitting beside him in a white tennis dress, her golden hair swept back like a plume by the breeze. They were probably returning from an afternoon at the country club. So that was the reason why Dan was so downhearted!

After dinner on Sunday, Mr. Payne drove his wife and the two girls over to see Big Black. Nancy tried to beg off, but her mother insisted that she be one of the family party.

Quite a crowd clustered before the new exhibit, and Professor Craig and his wife were among them. One look at the mounted bear put Oliver Payne in high spirits. Florence Craig and Karen delighted him with their admiration; Mrs. Payne remarked quietly upon the beauty of the exhibit. Nancy stood silently behind the others. Finally her stepfather turned to her with a hint of impatience.

"Well, Nancy, what do you think of this fellow? A lot of bear, eh?"

Just then Nancy noticed Alan Shelby standing back between two cases. He was looking at them with such an expression of bitter scorn on his strong-boned face that her cheeks burned scarlet with humiliation. Overwhelmed by a rush of sympathy for Alan, she bit back the meaningless polite words she had meant to say to her stepfather.

"He'd be a better-looking bear if he was alive!" she snapped and walked away.

Alan did not speak or look at Nancy as she passed him. She felt like crying, but she lifted her head proudly. If Alan was so narrow-minded as to include her in his hatred of her stepfather, then let him go. She wouldn't even allow herself to think of him any more.

At closing time on Tuesday, Dan Stevens lingered on the museum portico to chat with Miss May and Nancy. When the group broke up, he accompanied Nancy. "I'd like to drive you home," he offered abruptly.

Nancy looked at him in surprise. Remembering what a terrible driver he was, she opened her mouth to refuse his invitation and then, instead, heard herself saying, "That's nice of you, Dan." There was something so forlorn about him that she didn't have the heart to turn him down. She wondered if Lucille had tossed him aside altogether and was seeing only the fellow with the gorgeous white convertible.

As they walked toward the museum parking lot, Nancy glimpsed Alan's tall figure striding across the campus toward the May house. He must have seen her, too, but he didn't wave or show in any way that he was aware of her existence. Nancy turned to Dan and began to chatter gaily, but when they got out on the road in the little red car, she felt anything but gay.

"Must we go so fast?" she gasped, as Dan steered recklessly in and out through the traffic.

Dan laughed. "You're living in the jet age, kid," he reminded her.

It apparently wasn't in Dan to be a careful driver, and Nancy's heart was in her throat more than once during that drive. She sighed with relief when they turned into Orchard Road. *Never again!* she vowed to herself. But her troubles were not yet over. A short way up the road, they rounded a curve and there were Lucille and her new beau driving along in the white convertible. The red car put on a burst of speed and passed them with a roar, swaying crazily as it rounded the next curve. Nancy gasped. It seemed to her that her hair must be standing straight up on her head.

"The next driveway is ours," she croaked.

Dan slammed into the drive and bounced to a stop near the house. For a moment Nancy could not speak; then she said faintly, "Thanks for the ride. Will you come in for a glass of lemonade?"

Dan's face was sullen with unhappiness. "I'll take a

rain check on that," he told her. Then he added in a rush, "Nancy, will you go to a party with me tomorrow night?"

For a moment, Nancy was too surprised to answer. She bit her lip, thinking it over. She didn't really care about going out with Dan, but she also felt that it would be silly to spend the rest of the summer mooning over Alan Shelby.

"Do you know Doris Shaw?" Dan was saying. "She lives on Highland Drive, not far from here. It's her party. I'd like you to go with me."

"I'd have to be home by eleven," Nancy murmured, still not quite sure that she wanted to go.

"That's OK," Dan said.

"Then I'll ask my mother and tell you tomorrow at the museum," Nancy promised without enthusiasm. But Dan did not appear to notice.

Getting her mother's permission to go to the party was no trouble at all. Mrs. Payne was acquainted with Mrs. Shaw, and the fact that Dan was employed at the museum vouched for him.

"You see?" Mrs. Payne said, delighted that Nancy had found a new friend. "I told you there were more attractive young men in the world than that wild boy from Maine!"

Nancy sighed to herself and did not reply.

When Nancy arrived at the museum the next day, Alan was trimming the shrubs around the portico. She hesitated on the top step and glanced at him, but Alan ignored her and the pruning shears continued their busy clicking. Nancy tossed her head and flounced into the museum, her cheeks burning and tears blinding her eyes. But she had to admit to herself that she had invited the snub. Alan had plainly shown that he wanted nothing to do with Oliver Payne's stepdaughter, and if she had any pride at all, she'd never look at him again!

To Nancy's relief, Dan did not offer to drive her home that night, but promised to call for her about eight to take her to the party. After dinner, she went to her room and inspected the contents of her closet. Her only real party frock was the one her mother had bought her for the museum banquet, and going out with Dan Stevens didn't seem to be a gala enough occasion for that lovely dress. She gave the filmy white skirt a satisfied little pat and then took down her red calico print.

Karen lounged on the bed with the little stuffed tiger, watching Nancy get ready for the party.

"You look sweet," she said, "but my pearl earrings are just the touch you need for that dress."

She dashed into her room and came back with her cultured pearl earrings, small drops dangling from small buttons. To please her, Nancy screwed them on and then decided that they looked quite nice.

The doorbell rang as Nancy was going downstairs. Karen peeked over the balustrade to get a glimpse of her date while Nancy ran down the last few steps to open the door. Dan stood there smiling pleasantly and looking very sharp in light summer suit.

"Come in," Nancy greeted him. "I'll just say good-by to Mother."

But now both Mr. and Mrs. Payne came into the hall.

Nancy introduced Dan rather stiffly, for this was the first time a boy had called for her. She could tell from her mother's cordial manner that Dan had made a good impression. Mr. Payne beamed and reminded Dan in a jolly voice that there was an eleven o'clock curfew for his girls.

"Drive carefully," he added, following them out to the porch.

If you only knew! thought Nancy.

But perhaps because he was awed by her stepfather, Dan got under way smoothly and drove sedately down the drive. Nancy sat beside him, making no effort at conversation.

Why did she feel depressed, rather than elated, at starting out on this date? She scarcely noticed when they swung into Orchard Road and Dan roared away with his usual recklessness.

"Doris is a friend of Lucille's," Dan explained a little later, as he turned the little car into Highland Drive. "When she invited me to this party, Lucille and I were almost engaged. Now Lucille has taken up with a new guy."

Nancy felt a stab of apprehension. She was a perfect stranger to Doris Shaw. Would Doris want or expect Dan to bring a stranger to her party? Would she even expect him to come himself, now that he and Lucille had broken up?

"Dan . . ." she began.

But Dan was busy finding a parking place among the many cars on the road in front of a spacious, new ranch-type house.

"Come on—come on," he urged, when Nancy lingered in the car.

He pulled the door open and Nancy got out slowly. She stood smoothing her full skirt and gazing doubtfully at the house. Dan tucked his hand beneath her elbow and propelled her up the flagstone walk. His ring was answered by a pretty brunette girl in a dressy pink silk dress. Nancy took one look and realized that her red print was not right for this party.

A fleeting expression of surprise crossed Doris Shaw's face when she saw who the new arrivals were; then her good manners took over and she welcomed them cordially. But that instant of hesitation had been enough to make Nancy feel decidedly uncomfortable. Now she was certain that Doris had not expected Dan to turn up at her party—and certainly not to bring a strange girl.

Resentment surged through Nancy. She told herself that she would never forgive Dan for putting her in such an embarrassing situation. She longed to rush out of the house and run away down the road, but, instead, she must stay here, stuck with Dan for the evening and sick with the realization that she was an unwanted, even though politely welcomed guest.

The party was in full swing on the patio. A record player was spilling out the latest hit tune. Some couples were dancing while others sat about chatting gaily. Nancy saw that all of them were years older than she. Doris urged Dan to get Cokes for Nancy and himself, and then she hurried away to dance with her date. Dan was searching through the crowd with eager eyes, but

Lucille's golden hair was nowhere to be seen. He looked keenly disappointed as he turned to Nancy.

"Let's dance," he said without enthusiasm, sliding his arm around her.

He was a good dancer, but Nancy could not get into a dancing mood—especially after she heard one young man say to his date, "Where did the kid come from?"

"Even Doris would like to know." The girl giggled.

Nancy longed to sink through the brick patio floor. Why, oh why, had she ever allowed herself to go out on a date with Dan?

A stir near the doorway announced some new arrivals. A girl's voice trilled, "Hello, everybody. I guess most of you know Ray Williams, here."

It was Lucille with her handsome new beau. To Nancy's embarrassment, Dan stopped dancing and stood with his arm about her, but with his eyes, all his heart in them, staring at the girl who had just stepped out of the house.

There was no denying that Lucille was beautiful. The prettiness of the other girls paled in contrast to the glow of her beauty. Her golden hair was swept high tonight, and it shimmered richly in the light of the electric lanterns hung about the patio. Her sleeveless dress of turquoise-blue matched her eyes in color. She was all gold and blue, except for the luscious pink of her smiling lips. And her escort was a perfect foil for her—tall, romantically dark, handsome as a movie star.

Doris hurried over to welcome her friend. She whispered something to her, and then both of them looked at Dan and Nancy. Lucille's arched eyebrows went up, and she bestowed a wave of her hand and a dazzling smile on Dan. Dan stared back at her like a penniless kid with his nose pressed against the window of a candy store.

Oh dear, Nancy thought, if he just wouldn't let her know how he feels!

Pity for lovesick Dan wiped out her former resentment. She realized now that he had brought her to the party only because he wanted to be near Lucille and felt that he needed a partner. Although Nancy felt humiliated, she was sorry for him. It would have been difficult for him to face Lucille and her date without having a date of his own.

Lucille and Ray began to dance, and Dan started to move again. Not that one could call it dancing! It was more like stepping about to music with a man in a trance. Lucille gave Dan a melting glance as they passed, and Dan stumbled and lost the beat. Nancy was thankful when Mrs. Shaw came out on the patio and announced that refreshments were served.

It was a buffet supper. A table laden with delicious food was spread in the dining room, off which the patio opened, and the young people served themselves. Nancy didn't feel hungry, but she put a dab of salad and a roll on her plate. She noticed that the other young men were waiting on their dates, but Dan just stood watching Lucille. Anger and humiliation began to edge out Nancy's sympathy for him. He had brought her to this party and the least he could do was to show her token courtesy!

Dan followed Lucille and Ray back to the patio, and Nancy tagged unhappily along. Under half-lowered lids, as she toyed with her salad, Nancy studied Lucille's new beau. He was well aware of his good looks, and he had a roving eye for other girls, too. Lucille would have done better to have stuck with Dan, Nancy decided. Oh, why had she come to this party? She didn't have a thing in common with anyone there. She chuckled to herself as she pictured how Lucille's handsome escort would react if she should attempt to engage him in conversation about Archelon or Stegosaurus.

Ray Williams got into flirtatious chit-chat with a girl who was sitting nearby. Lucille's eyes began to glitter and her smile became strained. The beauty was jealous! Suddenly she turned to Dan with that melting look.

"Where have you been keeping yourself, Danny?"

"Near the telephone," he answered promptly. "You promised to call."

She gave a tinkling little laugh. "I've been so busy . . ."

Both of them were oblivious to Nancy. Lucille glanced at her date. He had taken the other girl's hand and was examining a ring she was wearing. Lucille lifted her golden head proudly and turned back to Dan. Just then someone started the music again.

"We could dance this one together, Dan," Lucille murmured.

Dan jumped to his feet and seized Lucille's hand to pull her up. Nancy stared after them in rising indignation as they danced away. Dan had forgotten her very existence! She heard an angry mutter from Lucille's date as he stood up and prepared to cut in. Of course, that was just what Lucille hoped he would do! Suddenly Nancy felt that she just had to get away from the whole silly business.

She stood up and moved quietly around the edge of the patio. In the dining room she found Mrs. Shaw. "I don't feel very well," she told her. "I think I had better go home. It's been a lovely party," she added dutifully.

"You came with Dan Stevens, didn't you?" Mrs. Shaw asked. "Is he going to drive you home?"

Nancy hadn't considered how she was going to get home, only that she was going.

"Dan is having such a good time, I thought I'd just slip away without telling him," she said hastily.

Was there a knowing light in Mrs. Shaw's eyes? "But, my dear, you can't go home alone," she protested.

"I'll call my stepfather and he'll come right over," Nancy told her, eager to get away.

The woman looked relieved. "Oh, yes, of course, you live quite near, on Orchard Road. You'll find the phone in the hall. Be sure to let me know if Mr. Payne can't come, and I'll have one of the boys drive you."

"He'll come," Nancy said confidently.

Glad to be allowed to go without any more fuss, she hurried out to the hall. She reached for the telephone and then hesitated. Did she want her family to know that she had been stood up, so to speak, by Dan Stevens? She turned resolutely away from the telephone and walked out of the house. Orchard Road wasn't so far away—she could walk home in a short time.

8

A pledge of friendship

Nancy set off briskly along Highland Drive and soon
the music of Doris Shaw's party faded behind her.
There were no sidewalks; she had to walk at the edge of
the road, and she was unprepared to find it such a dark
and lonely walk. She turned into another road, hoping
that she had chosen the one that led to Orchard Road,
for this part of the neighborhood was unfamiliar to her.
Now she almost regretted her impulsiveness in striking
out by herself—she might get lost and wander about for
hours!

Street lights were few here in the suburbs. Many of
the widely spaced houses were set in woodsy groves.
Others had long stretches of lawn, so that their lights
seemed to twinkle from far away. Fortunately it was a
clear and starry night. Nancy shivered a little and
wished that she had worn a sweater.

It was farther than she remembered to Orchard Road.
A rustle in the bushes beside the road startled her; then
a rabbit tore across the road. Nancy gave a low chuckle

over her momentary feeling of fear. A little farther on, she saw a big cat sitting on a stone gatepost.

"Hi, kitty!" she called softly.

The cat jumped down and walked with her a little way; then it turned aside to melt into the leafy shadows. Nancy bade it farewell with regret. The cat had been a more congenial companion than the people she had met at Doris Shaw's party!

She thought about that as she strode along through the starlit night. It was natural to want to have dates and go to parties. But, although Dan Stevens had seemed a likable person—or maybe it would be more apt to say that he was a person whose troubles had awakened her sympathy—she had known when she made the date that she and Dan had nothing in common except that they both worked at the museum. She had used Dan because she wanted to go out, just as he had used her because he needed a date for the party. After this, she decided, it would be more sensible to stay home unless she really cared about the person who asked her out. Otherwise how could she expect to have anything but a dull, uncomfortable time?

Walking with her easy stride, she drew a deep breath of the cool night air, feeling suddenly buoyant and de- lightfully self-sufficient. How brightly the stars were twinkling above the treetops! The Milky Way looked like a swarm of diamond bees. Fireflies were swinging their little lanterns in the woods and across the lawns. And here was Orchard Road at last.

There was more traffic on this road. Nancy stepped far over to the side as a car sped past. Probably the people in it were wondering how a girl happened to be walking by herself at that time of night. Nancy began to worry about getting into the house without having her mother discover that she had walked home from the party.

Headlights flashed around a bend in the road and another car came toward her. Nancy blinked in the glare. Her heart gave a frightened lurch as the car slowed and came to a stop. She had to pass it! She walked faster. Oh, she should have called Mr. Payne after all!

The car door opened. Someone was getting out! Should she run? Nancy wondered wildly. Then a familiar voice called out, "Nancy, what in the world are you doing on the road at this hour?"

It was Alan Shelby! Relief and gladness flooded over Nancy. She crossed the road to him.

"Oh, Alan, I'm so glad it's you!"

He opened the door of the station wagon for her. "Get in. I'll drive you home."

Nancy slid thankfully into the seat. She wriggled her toes in her party shoes, which certainly had not been designed for hiking.

Alan drove on until he came to a driveway; then he turned the station wagon around and started back toward the Payne house.

"Are you in the habit of taking walks by yourself at night?" he asked.

"I'm running away from a party," Nancy confessed.

After the way Alan had treated her, pride should have prevented her from accepting his offer of a ride, she told herself severely. But in spite of herself, she felt as much drawn to this boy as she was indifferent to Dan. She found it quite natural to tell him about her humiliating experience at the party. Probably an experienced girl like Lucille would never, never let one boy know that another had not found her utterly fascinating, but instinct told Nancy that the only firm basis for the kind of friendship she wanted with Alan was complete honesty.

"I ought to punch that Stevens' nose," Alan growled. Delighted that he felt so strongly about it, Nancy hastened to assure him that Dan had hurt only her pride.

"So let's forget him," said Alan. He turned his car into the Payne driveway and stopped in the shadow of the laurels.

"Know what I've been doing?" he asked gruffly. "I've been riding up and down Orchard Road for no reason except that you live here."

Nancy was astonished. Her heart began to beat a little faster.

"I wanted to apologize for my rudeness and ask you to be friends again," Alan continued. "But I didn't know how to get to you without alerting the rest of the family, and I can't imagine Papa Payne forming himself into a welcoming committee if he saw me driving up to his door."

Nancy giggled. "You're not very popular with my family," she agreed.

"How about you?" asked Alan.

"I've never stopped being your friend," she said softly.

"Let's shake on it then."

Their hands met in a warm clasp and clung together.

"I've never met a girl I liked as well as you, Nancy."

A glow of happiness lifted Nancy's spirits to the stars, but Alan's next words brought her down to earth again. "I don't give a darn if you *are* Oliver Payne's stepdaughter."

Nancy gently drew her hand away. Oh, if only Mr. Payne didn't have to be in the picture! But he was. He was her mother's husband and he had to be considered, no matter how entirely she was on Alan's side in the matter of Big Black.

"Alan," she said with a note of entreaty in her voice, "my mother is afraid that you came to Glendale Falls to take some sort of vengeance on Mr. Payne because of Big Black. I don't believe it for a minute, but I'd like to hear you say it."

There was a long moment of silence. Nancy's eyes, accustomed to the darkness now, studied Alan's firm profile, which wore an obstinate expression as he stared moodily through the windshield. She waited anxiously. "Alan?"

"OK, OK," he said sulkily. "You can set your mother's fears at rest. I'm not planning to bushwhack your precious stepfather. Does that satisfy you?"

"Of course. And, Alan, I want you to know that I don't blame you a bit for hating Mr. Payne. It was a horrible thing that he did. But Miss May says that we only hurt ourselves when we hate people," she added earnestly.

He turned to her with a shrewd look. "I don't believe that you're much sold on that stepfather of yours, are you, Nancy?"

"I want my mother to be happy, so I try to like Mr. Payne. I really do."

Alan leaned over and planted a kiss at the corner of her mouth.

"Oh!" Nancy cried. She pressed her fingers to the place.

"You're a sweet kid, Nancy."

Suddenly she remembered the time. "I must go in before Mother starts phoning the Shaws."

She pushed the car door open. Alan got out to help her.

"You don't dare drive up to the door in my wagon," he accused her.

Nancy gave a low laugh. All of a sudden she found life delightfully exhilarating. The pledge of friendship with Alan, her first kiss, and the romantic meeting with him under the stars all added up to something infinitely exciting and satisfying. She ran up the drive toward the house, turning once to wave.

"See you tomorrow," Alan called after her.

Nancy was on the house steps when her mother opened the door.

"Well, Nancy, it's almost midnight," Mrs. Payne said severely. "I don't wonder that the young man was afraid to drive you up to the door."

Thankful that her mother didn't know which young man had brought her home, Nancy went inside. Through the doorway to the living room she could see Mr. Payne reading in his favorite chair. He raised his head to give her a half-smile.

"It's a little later than you were supposed to be home," he reminded her mildly.

Nancy walked silently to the staircase. It was hard to take even so gentle a reprimand from her stepfather.

Her mother shook her head. "Did you have a good time at the party?" she asked.

Nancy paused and gave her an almost bemused glance. She had all but forgotten the party. The slights she had suffered seemed faraway and unimportant now.

"It wasn't much fun," she admitted. "My dress wasn't right . . ."

"Oh, dear." Her mother sighed.

"And the others were older. They acted as if Dan had brought someone from the kindergarten."

"I'm so sorry, dear, that the evening turned out badly." Her mother looked very much concerned. "But there will be other parties . . ."

Suddenly Nancy felt ashamed of the impulse to deceive her mother. Until now, everything had been in the open between them and she wasn't going to allow her friendship with Alan to change this.

"The party was just awful, Mother," she burst out. "Dan forgot me completely when his old girl showed up, and I—well, I ran away and walked home."

Her mother gasped. "You walked home from Highland Drive at this time of night?" Her sharp tone brought Mr. Payne into the hall.

"Why didn't you call me if you wanted to come home?" he asked Nancy.

"I didn't mind walking."

"But I saw the headlights of a car in the drive." Nancy's mother was very much upset. "You didn't allow some stranger to pick you up on the road, Nancy?"

"No, Mother. It was Alan Shelby. He just happened to be driving along Orchard Road when I came by. He drove me the rest of the way."

"That boy again!" Mrs. Payne exclaimed.

Mr. Payne's interest had quickened at the mention of Alan. "Now why should Shelby just happen to be driving along Orchard Road?" he demanded. "What business does he have out here?"

"How should I know?" Nancy cried impatiently.

"Some mischief, I'll be bound," Mr. Payne said with deep suspicion.

"I told you not to associate with that wild boy!" cried Nancy's mother.

Nancy felt buffeted between the two of them. "He only drove me home. And he's a nice boy—truly he is, Mother." Her voice rang defiantly. "I like him and I'm glad he wants to be my friend."

"Nancy!" Mrs. Payne made an obvious effort to control her anger.

"He told me that he has no intention of doing anything to Mr. Payne," Nancy hurried on. "I believe him. You would too, Mother, if you'd only talk to him."

"I have no desire to talk to the Shelby boy. I know that he hates your father, and if you had any loyalty in you, Nancy . . ."

Something in Nancy's face caused Mr. Payne to lay his hand on his wife's arm.

"Let Nancy go to bed now, my dear. She's home safe, and that's all that matters."

Nancy turned and ran upstairs, seething with hurt because Mr. Payne had had to intercede for her with her mother. Halfway up, she paused and looked back. Her mother was standing with her hand on the newel post, looking as much disturbed as Nancy felt. Nancy ran down again and kissed her fiercely.

"Good night, Mother. Good night, Mr. Payne," she added to please her mother.

Karen was waiting to hear about the party and she called out as Nancy passed. Obviously Karen had not heard any of the conversation that had taken place in the lower hall. Nancy was grateful for this.

She unscrewed the pearl earrings and laid them on Karen's dressing table. "You were a duck to let me wear them."

"Did you have fun?" Karen asked eagerly. She was sitting up in bed with her arms clasped around her knees. "It must be fun to go out with an older crowd. All the girls think Doris Shaw is simply terrific."

"She's nice," Nancy agreed. "But I don't have anything in common with her or her friends. I won't be going out with them again."

"Oh!" Karen looked sympathetic. "I guess Dan was too sophisticated for you. But never mind, you'll meet lots of cute boys at school next fall."

"Uh-huh." Nancy was glad to let it go at that.

Nancy was entirely unprepared for the commotion which she walked into when she went downstairs the next morning.

Mr. Payne was standing in the lower hall, looking very angry. His wife, Karen, and Minnie Bell were gathered around him, twittering like a flock of excited birds. Mr. Payne glared at Nancy.

"So that young rascal, Alan Shelby, 'just happened' to be driving along Orchard Road last night!" he shouted.

Nancy stood still and tense at the foot of the stairs. "I don't know what you're talking about."

"I'll tell you what I'm talking about! Someone broke into my garage last night and slashed every tire on my car."

"It wasn't Alan," Nancy said firmly.

"I don't agree with you, Nancy. It was that boy's way of getting even with me because of Big Black."

"Alan wouldn't do a vicious thing like that."

"Then what was he doing in this neighborhood?" her stepfather demanded.

"He wanted to see me," Nancy said bravely.

"Nancy," her mother put in sternly, "I've had just about enough nonsense over that boy. He came to Glendale Falls nursing a grudge against your father, and last night he came sneaking around to see what damage he could do . . ."

"Alan's not a sneak!" Nancy burst out. "Is there any proof that he's the one who slashed the tires?"

"No. But who else . . ."

"He *didn't* do it. You're all prejudiced against him."

Her words only served to anger her mother. "You're not to go to the museum today, or ever while that boy is there."

Nancy was stunned. Tears flooded her eyes and rolled down her cheeks. Her beloved job! She turned and hid her face against the newel post. As at a great distance, she heard her stepfather say, "Karen, go and eat your breakfast! Minnie, pour my coffee!"

When Karen and the housekeeper had unwillingly left the hall, Mr. Payne stepped to Nancy's side. "Nancy," he said, "you really do believe in Alan Shelby, don't you?"

She lifted her head and wiped away her tears with the back of her hand. She sniffed, tried to speak, then simply nodded.

Oliver Payne gave her a thoughtful glance, and then he turned to his wife.

"Amy, I want you to allow Nancy to continue at the museum. It scarcely seems right to punish her for being loyal to a friend."

Mrs. Payne hesitated while Nancy held her breath. "Very well," she said at last. "But Nancy, there is to be no driving about with that boy. No dates. Do you understand?"

Nancy nodded, biting her lips to steady their trembling. The hurt went deep that Mr. Payne again had had to champion her cause with her mother.

"Now let's have breakfast." Mr. Payne shooed his wife and stepdaughter into the dining room, where brimming bowls of Payne's Krispys awaited them. He ate hastily and then walked around the table to kiss his wife good-by. "I'm sorry to be forced to borrow your car this morning, dear. I'll send a man over with some new tires for mine. And I'll stop by the police station to report what happened here last night. They may be able to help us locate the culprit."

"May I be excused, Mother?" Nancy asked.

"I suppose so. But, dear, you've hardly touched your breakfast! Have one of Minnie's blueberry muffins."

"They're scrumptious," Karen said, buttering her second one.

Nancy shook her head and got to her feet. She was afraid that if she lingered, Alan's name would be brought up again. Her mother reached out and grasped her hand.

"It's for your own sake, Nancy, that I'm concerned about your association with that Shelby boy."

"I know, Mother," Nancy answered wearily. "But you're wrong about Alan. Someday you'll see."

There was a dejected look about her as she walked out of the room. For the first time in her life she had met a boy with whom she wanted to be friends and who seemed to like her as much as the liked him, and of all the boys in the world it had to be one her mother detested!

9

The topaz necklace

It was the police who cleared Alan of the suspicion of
having slashed the tires. When Mr. Payne called at the
police station, they told him that a gang of boys had
been committing similar acts of vandalism around the
city, apparently just for kicks. Several of the young
gangsters had been rounded up, and the police were trying to trace the others. When Mr. Payne told the story at
the dinner table that night, he appeared to be genuinely
pleased that Alan had been vindicated.

"We were too hasty. I'm sorry we wronged the boy."

Mrs. Payne nodded, but without much enthusiasm.
"I still think that the boy's motive for coming to Glen-
dale Falls had something to do with you and that bear,
Oliver."

Nancy sighed to herself. She could not contradict her
mother this time, because deep inside her there lurked
the same conviction.

The rest of the family began to talk about the midsummer banquet of the Museum Associates, which was

to take place the following Tuesday. Nancy had heard just today that Alan would be attending the banquet as Miss May's escort, but she did not share this information with the rest of the family.

Mr. Payne had stopped at the bank and brought home his grandmother's topaz necklace. Before locking it in the bedroom safe, he opened the case and showed the jewels to the two girls. The stones glittered like drops of molten sunshine against the background of black velvet. Between each topaz was set a diamond, and in the center, a large pear-shaped topaz of clearest water hung as a pendant.

"Oh, how lovely!" Nancy exclaimed.

Under her father's smiling eyes, Karen scooped up the necklace and held it high to flash and sparkle in the light.

"It will look gorgeous on your mother," Mr. Payne said, with a fond glance at his wife. "It takes a beautiful woman to give added luster to a handsome piece of jewelry."

The museum closed early on Tuesday. The banquet was to be held in the huge, air-conditioned Hall of Dinosaurs, and the caterer needed time to make his arrangements. On her way out of the building, Nancy almost bumped into Dan Stevens, who came flying down the stairs in all his old time flurry. He gave her a shamefaced look. He had avoided her since the night of Doris Shaw's party.

"I'm sorry about the other night, Nancy," he said

humbly. "I—well, you must have guessed how it is with me about Lucille."

"I understand, Dan. It's all right." Nancy found it easy to forgive his rudeness because she didn't care any more. And since he didn't ask how she had reached home, it was obvious that he was indifferent.

And he's the one whom Mother calls "A nice young man!" Nancy thought bitterly.

"Are you coming to the banquet tonight, Dan?" she asked, for want of something to say.

"Yep. And Lucille is coming with me. Be seeing you," he added as he took off. "I've got to pick her up at the hairdresser."

So Lucille was going out with Dan again! In spite of herself, Nancy felt sorry for Dan. Why couldn't he see that Lucille was probably just using him to make Ray Williams jealous?

At home, Nancy was caught up in the pleasurable flurry of getting ready for the banquet, which was one of the big social events of Glendale Falls. This time Nancy had no fear that her dress would not be right for the occasion. She took it out of the closet and laid it carefully on the bed. Exquisite in its simplicity, it was made of delicate white material, sleeveless, and with a round neck and a swirl of skirt that hung in soft folds beneath a wide, emerald-green belt.

Nancy took a shower and put on the lingerie of fine batiste and lace that her mother had bought for her to wear with this dress. Next she put on her emerald-green slippers, and then the dress. She started to zip herself up the back, but then danced into Karen's room to ask for assistance.

"I was just coming to ask you for help." Karen chuckled.

She zipped Nancy's dress and then whirled around so that Nancy could perform the same service for her. Her dress was shell-pink in color. The two girls made a pretty picture as they stood together before Karen's mirror.

"Come see my dress, girls!" Mrs. Payne called from down the hall. Nancy and Karen joined her in the big front bedroom. "How do you like me?" She pivoted before them, gay as a girl in her dress of cream-colored lace, cut with a low V neckline. The girls expressed their admiration of both her and the gown.

Mr. Payne was standing by the dressing table with the jewel case open beside him. Now he picked up the topaz necklace and stepped over to put it around his wife's neck. Against her white-rose skin, it flashed with barbaric splendor.

"Lovely—lovely!" Karen cried.

Her father beamed proudly. Mrs. Payne turned to look at herself in the mirror. She touched the jewels almost timidly.

"Oliver," she murmured. "It's too gorgeous—it overwhelms me."

"Nonsense! You look magnificent. Isn't that right, girls?"

Both girls hastened to agree. But Nancy sensed how her mother felt. The topaz necklace was overwhelming in its splendor.

Professor and Mrs. Craig were in the entrance hall of the museum to receive the guests. With them was Hank Rawlings, the big-game hunter. Mr. Payne immediately began to tell him about Big Black.

"Wait until you see him!" he boasted. "That Alaskan grizzly you wrote about in your last book couldn't have been more of a thrill to see over the sights of your rifle than this big one."

Nancy moved away so that she would hear no more. She had read that grizzly bears were becoming extinct because they had been hunted so relentlessly. Why did some men take such joy in killing? She glanced back at her stepfather and Mr. Rawlings, sleek and urbane in their dinner jackets. They were supposed to be civilized men, yet in their lust to kill animals, had they really advanced beyond the men of cave times? And had even cave men killed for pleasure? They must have needed all their skill merely to hunt for food!

"Why are you so deep in thought?"

Alan was suddenly standing beside Nancy. He was wearing a light summer dinner jacket, a dark bow tie, and dark trousers. He grinned as he noticed her look of surprise.

"This outfit belongs to Burton Payne," he confessed. "I came to the banquet with Miss May and him. I had nothing fit to wear, but they fixed me up. Burton is a swell fellow. But what were you pondering so deeply when we came in?"

"I was contrasting modern civilized man with the hunters of the cave era."

Alan's eyes followed hers to where Mr. Payne and

Mr. Rawlings were deep in talk. "Yeah, I know what you mean," he muttered.

Miss May and Burton Payne had stopped near the entrance to chat with friends. Now they walked toward the receiving line. Nancy saw Cousin Burton start and halt suddenly, his narrowed eyes upon her mother's necklace. The topazes and diamonds caught the light from the great chandelier overhead and flung it back a hundredfold. What a shock it must have been for Burton suddenly to see the necklace! Miss May had noticed it too now, and there was dismay in her face. Nancy wondered nervously if Cousin Burton was going to make a scene that would embarrass her mother. But he seemed to pull himself together. He ignored Mr. Payne, but his greetings to the rest of the group were cordial.

"It was most indiscreet to flaunt that necklace before Burton," Miss May murmured to Nancy.

"Mother couldn't help it," Nancy declared. "I don't think she even likes the old necklace. It's too bad someone doesn't steal it."

"I doubt whether there are any jewel thieves here tonight." Miss May changed the subject. "How pretty you look, Nancy."

"You too," Nancy returned.

The older woman was handsome in her periwinkle-blue dinner gown, and there was a happy glow about her. Burton Payne took her arm possessively. His sharp eyes softened and twinkled whenever he looked at her.

Mrs. Payne looked around and frowned slightly when she saw Alan beside Nancy. She made a little motion for Nancy to join the family.

"My mother wants me," said Nancy. "It must be almost time for the banquet to begin."

"Any chance of me getting to drive you home afterward?" Alan asked.

"I guess not." Nancy sighed. "Mother's still afraid that you're plotting something against Mr. Payne."

"Oh, for Pete's sake!" Alan gave an exasperated groan. "Why did you have to be Oliver Payne's stepdaughter?"

"Why indeed?" Nancy murmured as she moved away.

"Is that Alan?" Karen whispered when Nancy joined the family group. Nancy nodded. "He's a doll," Karen said, with her pixie smile. "I don't believe he's as bad as they say."

"Come, girls," Mrs. Payne said, as she moved off with her husband.

The crowd of well-dressed people, men in dinner jackets and women in pastel summer gowns, was flowing toward the Hall of Dinosaurs. Nancy gave a little gasp of delight when she stepped through the doorway. Was there ever a more unusual and romantic setting for a banquet?

The great hall was lighted by ceiling lights. In this soft glow the weirdly beautiful murals on the walls, with their exotic cinnamon trees, feathery tree ferns, great fig trees, and dark laurels, took on a dreamlike quality through which the awesome reptiles of the distant past moved like dragons in fairy tales.

The caterer had arranged his round, damask-covered tables among the exhibits in the hall. Candles shone like stars, silverware gleamed, and a subtle fragrance

came from the snapdragons and ferns in the center-
pieces. Professor and Mrs. Craig, Mr. Rawlings, and
the President of Glendale College sat at the table at the
end of the hall, with the stegosaurus looming up in the
background. The Payne family had a table nearby;
so did Burton Payne and his party. Farther away,
Nancy saw Dan Stevens and Lucille, Lucille looking
stunning in red chiffon with her golden hair piled high.
She was staring at Mrs. Payne's necklace, envy plain
upon her face.

The meal was delicious, but Nancy felt too uneasy to
enjoy her food. It seemed that every time she glanced
at Cousin Burton at the next table, he was staring at the
topaz necklace with sparks of fire in his eyes. Then she
got to wondering how Alan would react when Mr.
Payne took Hank Rawlings to see Big Black. He looked
moody enough to be planning something drastic!

Deft waiters cleared the dessert away, and Professor
Craig introduced Mr. Rawlings as the speaker of the
evening. Mr. Rawlings' talk was spirited and witty and
he made big-game hunting sound like a thrilling, sports-
manlike activity. He told his audience that limited
hunting would keep the wildlife population down to
numbers that could be safely supported by the dwin-
dling wild lands of the globe. This was the other side of
the picture, but it left Nancy cold. She did not raise her
hands from her lap when Mr. Payne led the applause.

Now Mr. Payne had the guest of honor by the arm
and was urging him toward the corridor that led to the
Hall of Wildlife. The other guests trailed them as they
started off, but everyone stopped to admire the stego-

saurus and a large throng jammed that end of the hall. Mr. Payne finally got the procession moving again. Alan jostled Nancy and her mother in the crowd, as he dropped to the rear. He muttered an apology, then bent to pick up the souvenir menu that Nancy had dropped. His face was set grimly, and Nancy knew that he was thinking about Big Black. She stepped back from her mother and slipped away, too.

"Alan!" she called softly.

He turned and waited near Archelon.

"I don't want to be there either to hear him boast about shooting Big Black," she said when she reached Alan's side. He reached for her hand. Silently, close together, they walked out of the Hall of Dinosaurs, where the caterer's men were already moving chairs and tables out through the firedoor. In the entrance hall, they climbed the marble stairs and sat down midway to the landing. Below them, some of the guests had started to leave.

"You'll get in trouble for being with me," Alan teased.

Nancy sighed. "If only we could convince my mother that you didn't come to Glendale Falls to take some gruesome vengeance on Mr. Payne."

"It's not vengeance I want," Alan said grimly. A lock of his dark hair had fallen over his forehead, giving him a reckless appearance. "But your stepfather is going to find out that he can't make an exhibition of Big Black for his own glory."

"Alan!" Nancy was startled. "What are you planning to do?"

"You'll see! Everyone will see! I don't care if I go to

jail . . ." He broke off abruptly, as if he were conscious of having said too much.

Nancy felt apprehensive. After her stout defense of him, Alan was planning some wild scheme that might put him in jail! She searched frantically for the right words.

"Alan, whatever you're planning to do won't bring Big Black back. I just can't believe that you mean any harm to Mr. Payne!" she burst out.

Alan gave her a slow grin, but he didn't answer.

The people who had been looking at the habitat groups were now drifting back to the entrance hall. Oliver Payne was smiling broadly, so evidently Mr. Rawlings had been properly impressed by Big Black. Nancy knew a moment of relief, and she guessed that Mr. Payne felt the same, because, after all, Alan had not made a scene calculated to humiliate the man who had killed his bear.

From her high perch, Nancy noted that Lucille looked thoroughly bored as she strolled beside Dan. Karen had fallen in with a boy she knew, and they were laughing and exchanging banter. Mrs. Payne paused in the corridor doorway to glance around the entrance hall. Nancy stood up and Alan with her.

"I guess my mother wants to go now. Alan, please don't do anything rash."

He shook his head without answering.

People were milling about in the hall saying good night—and that it had been an outstanding banquet. Alan joined Miss May and Burton Payne. Nancy went to her mother. Mrs. Payne gave her a reproving shake of her head, then became conscious that Nancy was staring at her in a startled way.

"What is it, Nancy? Is something the matter?"

"Your necklace," said Nancy. "When did you take it off?"

"Take it off?" Mrs. Payne's hand flew to her throat. She gave a cry of dismay. "Oliver! I've lost the necklace!" She looked frightened.

Oliver Payne stepped quickly to his wife's side. "Now don't be upset," he told her. "The clasp is old—it must have given way and the necklace slipped off." He summoned Mr. Baron in his authoritive way. "Mrs. Payne has lost a valuable necklace. Please see that all the lights are turned on—then come with Professor Craig and me to search the halls."

His voice rang loudly in the crowded hall. People watched silently while the three men went back into the deserted Hall of Dinosaurs. After a moment, Burton Payne followed them.

Mr. Rawlings consulted his wrist watch. "I have a plane to catch," he told the President of Glendale College.

"Someone will drive you to the airport." The president glanced about anxiously. "Perhaps I'd better call a taxi."

"I'll be glad to drive Mr. Rawlings," Alan Shelby offered.

He spoke to Miss May and then accompanied Mr. Rawlings outside. Dan and Lucille and another couple left at the same time. The rest of the people waited until the four searchers returned to the hall.

"Did you find it?" Mrs. Payne asked her husband eagerly.

He shook his head dejectedly. Burton Payne, entering the hall behind the others, stepped over to his cousin and all but shook his fist in his face.

"You had to flaunt my necklace, didn't you?" His voice was choked with emotion. "And now you've succeeded in losing it. What are you going to do about it, eh?"

"Burton, please!" Miss May clasped the excited man's arm and drew him away.

Mrs. Payne started to cry. "Oh, Oliver, I'm so sorry." She pressed her lace handkerchief to her mouth.

Her husband patted her arm tenderly. "It wasn't your fault, dear. I should have checked that clasp."

For the first time, Nancy felt something akin to liking for her stepfather.

"We'd better call the police in on this," Mr. Payne continued. "Someone must have found the necklace on the floor and pocketed it."

Indignant denials came from the other guests present. However, Professor Craig used the telephone on Mr. Baron's desk to make the call. There was a police cruiser in the neighborhood of the museum and it was only a few minutes after the call that two officers walked into the hall. After listening to Mr. Payne's story, they made another careful search, but with no result. Returning to the entrance hall, one of the officers asked Professor Craig if he had a list of the people who had attended the banquet.

"I have a list of those who purchased tickets. Some brought guests . . ."

"And there were also the caterer's men—waiters and cleaning men, all of whom have now left the building," put in Burton Payne.

The policeman groaned as he wrote in this notebook. "Not a very large crowd here now," he observed. "I suppose quite a few have left?"

"Guests have been leaving ever since Mr. Rawlings and a young man started for the airport," admitted the college president.

"What young man?" Oliver Payne demanded.

His eyes darted around the hall. With a start, Nancy realized that he was looking for Alan. But surely he didn't believe that Alan had stolen the necklace!

"Where's young Shelby?" Mr. Payne asked sharply.

Nancy stepped close to his side. "He took Mr. Rawlings to the airport."

She was thankful that the two policemen were talking to Professor Craig. Mr. Payne must not be allowed to throw suspicion on Alan by naming him to the police!

"He *didn't* steal the necklace," she said firmly. "He was sitting on the stairs with me from the time the banquet ended until Mother came back to the hall."

"He's one person who had a motive," Mr. Payne muttered.

"He didn't steal it," Nancy insisted in a low, urgent voice. "I'm sure he didn't."

Mr. Payne scowled at her from under his heavy

brows. "Nancy," he said finally, "I'd be happy to have you for my friend." He walked away to join the policemen. Listening anxiously, Nancy did not hear him mention Alan's name as a suspect.

The policeman who had been writing thrust his notebook into his pocket. "Finding this thief seems pretty hopeless," he admitted to Mr. Payne. "We'll check pawn shops and suspected fences for stolen goods, in case the necklace turns up with one of them. But usually when a famous piece of jewelry like this necklace is stolen, the thief holds on to it for months before trying to sell it."

Nancy heard Florence Craig whisper to her cousin. "Oh, if only Oliver had been content to let that wretched necklace stay in the bank!"

"Or if only he had given it back to its rightful owner," Burton snapped.

The officers assured Mr. Payne that the list of banquet guests and the caterer's men would be carefully checked at headquarters to see whether anyone on it had a criminal record.

It was a sober family party that returned to the Payne house. Nancy, in the rear seat of the car with Karen, listened glumly while her mother and stepfather discussed Alan Shelby.

"Can you remember whether the boy was ever close enough to you to get his hands on the necklace?" Mr. Payne asked.

She considered a moment. "Why, yes. He bumped into me while we were all crowded around the stegosaurus."

Nancy groaned to herself. She remembered also that Alan had jostled them. But he hadn't taken the necklace—she knew he hadn't.

Her mother was not so sure. "I can't remember whether I was wearing the necklace at that time or not. I may have dropped it earlier and he picked it up. Oliver, it was a mistake not to mention his hatred of you to the police."

"No. I won't brand the boy as a thief without positive proof," Mr. Payne said firmly.

How strange, Nancy thought, that her stepfather should be so much more tolerant of her friend than her own mother was.

10

Storm over the museum

Miss May telephoned Nancy the following morning and invited her to luncheon.

"I have something to tell you," she hinted with a musical lilt in her voice.

"I'd love to come," Nancy replied.

But later, when she told her mother about the invitation, Mrs. Payne said flatly that she could not go.

"I won't insist that you give up your job at the museum, since it means so much to you, but I won't have you going to Miss May's house while that boy is there."

Nancy was aghast. "Mother! You don't mean I'm *never* to go to the house? What will Miss May think?"

"Tell her the reason," Mrs. Payne said calmly. "Or if you wish, I'll telephone her and tell her that I won't have you associating with that awful boy she has living there."

"Mother! You wouldn't! Alan is not an awful boy. If only you'd get to know him better . . ."

"I know him quite well enough," her mother assured

her. "Now call Miss May and tell her that you cannot come to lunch!"

Nancy's voice was husky with tears when she got Miss May on the telephone. "Mother won't let me go to your house while Alan is there. I'm so sorry, Miss May."

There was a moment of silence at the other end of the line; then she heard Miss May's soothing voice. "It's all right, Nancy. Don't be upset. I'll tell you my news at the museum."

Nancy hung up and leaned her head on her hand, sobbing. Her mother came out of the living room and stood beside her.

"Nancy, I can't understand why you're so fascinated by Alan. Quite aside from his vicious disposition, he seems like a very ordinary person to me."

Nancy brushed the tears off her cheeks. "That's because you don't know him, Mother. Even Mr. Payne is more tolerant of my friendship with Alan than you are."

Her mother looked hurt. "I'm thinking of your welfare, dear." A ring of bitterness came into her voice. "I'll be glad when that wretched boy goes back to Maine— unless he goes to prison first for stealing the Payne topazes!"

Nancy's green eyes sparked with anger over the unjust accusation. "He *didn't* steal them, Mother! Alan is as honest as you and I!"

"Here we are, actually quarreling over that boy!" her mother exclaimed. "Nancy, try to understand that I want you to have a *nice* boy friend, but not someone like . . ."

She broke off as Karen appeared at the top of the

stairs. Nancy was grateful to her for appearing just then, because she didn't have the heart to argue with her mother about Alan any more.

Miss May was at the museum shop when Nancy arrived. "I'm glad you're early," Miss May said. "Now I can tell you my news before people start coming in." Her hazel eyes had a soft glow and some new happiness had given her an aura of youth and beauty. Nancy smiled.

"I can almost guess what your news is."

Miss May laughed. "Were Burton and I that transparent last night? Well then, we're engaged all over again, and we plan to be married very soon."

Nancy kissed her. "I'm so happy for you—and Cousin Burton, too. It's like a romance out of a book . . ."

"Burton is giving up his apartment. We plan to live in my house, and we've invited Alan to stay on with us."

"For good?" Nancy cried, astonished.

"Yes, for good. Burton has taken a great liking to Alan. He wants him to go to school in Glendale Falls next winter and start college the following year."

"Oh, how wonderful for Alan!"

"Alan doesn't have strong home ties since his father remarried," Miss May continued. "He's going home in a few days to talk our plans over with his father and ask him to agree to let him stay on with us."

Well, this is amazing, Nancy thought.

Alan would be starting in Glendale High when she herself started in the fall! What would her mother have to say about that?

"Burton and John Craig are planning a new fossil-hunting expedition for next summer," Miss May told her. "Burton will be taking Alan as his assistant. I plan to go along, and I want you to be my guest, Nancy."

Nancy clasped her hands together at her throat. "Oh, Miss May—how simply way way out of this world! I hope I can go!"

"Maybe you can," Miss May said.

Pictures of Alan and herself exploring the desert and discovering some tremendous fossil flashed through Nancy's mind. Then the bright bubble burst in her face.

"Mother won't even let me lunch at your house with Alan. Imagine her giving permission for me to go on a long trip if he's one of the party!"

"Never fear, Nancy. Before next summer we'll find a way to get Alan into your mother's good graces." Miss May waved her hand airily and the light caught and splintered off the huge new diamond on her finger.

"Miss May, your ring!" Nancy gasped. "It's fabulous!"

The older woman laughed. "Burton was a little carried away when he picked it out. But I love it," she added.

Late that afternoon, Alan came into the museum and stopped at the shop. "I've come to pay Big Black a visit," he told Nancy.

She smiled at him, hoping that his good luck in having won the friendship of Burton Payne might have reconciled him a little to having Big Black in the museum. At that moment, there were no customers at the shop, so Nancy whisked around the end of the counter to walk along the corridor with Alan.

"Have any clues turned up as to what happened to your mother's necklace?" he asked. Nancy shook her head, glad that he didn't guess that her mother was suspicious of him. She hastened to change the subject.

"Miss May told me that you'll be going to Glendale High next fall, and that you're to be a permanent member of her family."

"Miss May and Burton Payne are swell people," Alan answered in an offhand manner.

Strangely, he did not appear to be at all elated over the upward swing in his fortunes. Nancy waited for him to say something about how pleasant it would be for them to be going to the same school. Instead, he told her in a low voice, "I'm going home in a day or two, Nancy, and—I probably won't come back."

She stared at him.

"Don't you think your father will consent to your living with Cousin Burton?" she asked, upset over the possibility that he might have to forgo his big chance of going to college.

"It's not that," he muttered, not looking at her. "Dad would be happy that I have the chance to go to college, but—well, something may turn up to cancel all those fine plans that Miss May and Burton have made for me."

"Oh, Alan, what *could* happen?" Nancy asked with a hint of impatience. Suddenly she felt as if Alan had withdrawn into some place of his own where she could not follow. Why did he have to be so mysterious? "I should think you'd be almost crazy with joy to have your dream of going to college suddenly about to come true. But you hardly seem to care."

They had reached Big Black's case, and Alan stood before it staring at the display. The bear looked as if he were alive, standing among the blueberry bushes with the rocky wooded ledges of his mountain domain behind him.

"He's magnificent," Nancy breathed.

"Yes, but he doesn't belong in this glass case." A closed, set expression had come over Alan's strong face.

"Alan, you shouldn't brood so about Big Black," Nancy burst out. "It's a shame, but he's here in the museum, and here he must stay."

Alan tightened his jaw and muttered something under his breath; then he turned on his heel and strode back toward the entrance hall. After a few steps he stopped and looked around. "So long, Nancy," he said softly and walked swiftly away from her.

Fear of something unknown, something she couldn't even guess at, filled Nancy's heart. Anger followed. Was there ever such another maddening boy as Alan Shelby? He had stared at that bear so much that he was beginning to act like a grumpy old bear himself.

Ruthie Webster came over to the Payne house to see Nancy that evening, bringing Violet with her.

"Violet seems to be in fine fettle," Nancy remarked, as she watched the turtle nibble a petunia in the flower border. "So I guess Barry was a faithful caretaker."

"Barry says you want to show me the skeleton of a

great big turtle at the museum," Ruthie said eagerly. "Is it much bigger than Violet?"

"It's as big as a—a garage. You never dreamed of such a turtle, Ruthie."

"I'll come to the museum tomorrow," the little girl said, her eyes alight. "Mama or Barry will drive me over, and I can come home with you, Nancy."

"That will be fine," said Nancy. "We'll get a soda before we take the bus, so tell your mother you may be a little late."

The next day was breathlessly hot and humid. The weather man had forecast severe thunderstorms for the following day and relief from the heat. As she walked down Orchard Road to the bus, Nancy thought wistfully of Karen and Barry, who were spending the day at the country club pool. She looked up at the towering thunderheads that were gathering in the sky and wondered if the storms would indeed hold off until tomorrow.

Miss May arrived at the shop looking pale and wan. Even Smilodon seemed wilted as he leaped heavily to his usual place on the window sill.

"I have a terrific headache," Miss May said with a tired sigh. "There seems to be hardly anyone coming in today, Nancy, so I wonder if you could manage the shop by yourself?"

"Of course." Nancy was delighted to be given the responsibility. "You go take a pill and lie down. My mother often has a headache in hot weather." She hesitated, then asked rather stiffly, "How is Alan?"

"Alan is planning to start for Maine directly after work tonight. He wouldn't have waited this long, but today is pay day." Miss May shook her head worriedly. "Something is troubling that boy. When he said good-by to me this noon, I almost had the feeling that he would not be back."

Nancy's heart tightened. I'll probably never see him again, she thought, remembering his "So long, Nancy." But why—why—why?

Miss May gratefully took her departure. Smilodon had fallen into a doze on the window sill. "Just let him out at closing time, Nancy, and he'll come home, 'wagging his tail behind him,' " she said before she left.

Outside, the smothering heat grew more intense. The sky was darkening to an ominous mass of purple clouds. Mr. Baron turned on all the lights as shadows gathered in the entrance hall and in the corridors and windowless halls. The few visitors in the museum started leaving early. Ruthie Webster arrived a little after four.

"Gosh, it's hot!" she exclaimed, her flushed face moist beneath her damp hair. "Mama says that if it storms, we're to take a taxi home and she'll pay for it."

Nancy glanced about. The museum seemed quite deserted. Burton Payne had finished his mural, and he no longer came in every day. Professor Craig had left early. Most of the staff were away on vacation, and the few who were on the job had left soon after the curator.

"Better close early," one of the men had advised Mr. Baron. "The weather forecast predicts the very dickens of a storm tonight."

Nancy asked Mr. Baron to keep an eye on the shop while she showed Ruthie the Hall of Dinosaurs. As the two girls crossed the entrance hall, Nancy, out of the corner of her eye, thought she saw a movement along the corridor leading to the Wildlife Hall. She turned her head swiftly, but the corridor stretched away, empty beneath its overhead lights. Nancy smiled thinly. She had been thinking so constantly about Alan that now she imagined she had seen him walking along an empty corridor.

She put her arm around Ruthie's shoulders as they stood in the wide doorway of the Hall of Dinosaurs. Tomorrow she was scheduled to make a talk to a group of girl scouts who were coming in from a nearby summer camp, so she was glad to practice on Ruthie this afternoon. She swept her free arm in a dramatic half-circle to take in the big hall with its scattered skeletons and colorful murals.

"These are the creatures who lived in North America a hundred million years and more ago. Some dinosaurs lived right here in New England—their footprints have been found on stones in the Connecticut River valley. The landscape was very different then." She turned Ruthie gently to face one of the murals. "Great swamps covered the land, there were ferns as large as trees . . ."

Ruthie studied the painting of a tyrannosaurus who was feasting on the much larger brontosaurus he had just killed with his long, jagged teeth.

"I'm glad they're gone," she said solemnly.

"So am I," Nancy said with a chuckle. "Man couldn't have existed in the same world with the giant reptiles. But the weather changed and the swamps dried up, and the dinosaurs couldn't get enough to eat. They became extinct millions of years before the first man appeared on earth, but their fossilized bones left a story in the rocks for brilliant scholars like Professor Craig and Burton Payne to read. These men have pieced the story together, and so we know just what the world was like in the days of the living dinosaurs."

She took Ruthie's hand and led her across to the huge upended skeleton of the prehistoric turtle.

"Meet Archelon, Violet's great-great and a million greats uncle."

Ruthie gasped. "Violet wouldn't make a bite for a turtle like this!" She stared enthralled at the tremendous skeleton.

"Archelon was a sea turtle," Nancy told her. "His bones were found in rock that was once the sandy bottom of a sea that washed from the Gulf of Mexico to the Arctic, and from our modern State of Kansas to the Rocky Mountains."

She sat down on a bench placed near the turtle and, while Ruthie listened eagerly, began the story, as she imagined it, of how Archelon had escaped from the lizard-headed sea serpent by hiding in the sand at the bottom of the sea. As she talked, Nancy's eyes strayed over the giant turtle skeleton standing stark and majestic under the ceiling lights. Suddenly she caught the glint of a tiny spark flashing from a high, shadowy niche, where one of the turtle's massive vertebrae was attached to its upper shell. Idly she looked again and then caught her breath sharply. That golden sparkle, where the light was caught by something hidden in the cavity, could be a topaz! A necklace of topazes, pushed hastily into the little recess by someone who had seen the jewels slide from her mother's neck and who had snatched them up and hidden them.

With a sick feeling Nancy remembered how Alan had jostled her mother in the crowd around the stegosaurus and how he had stooped to pick up her menu. Had he picked up the necklace at the same time? He had been standing near Archelon when she had overtaken him. For a boy as tall as Alan, it would have been easy to reach up and push the necklace into the turtle skeleton. There had been no one else at this end of the hall—everyone had been looking at the stegosaurus!

The next moment she was deeply ashamed of such thoughts. A fine friend she was! Alan wouldn't steal— not even to hurt Oliver Payne. And certainly he wouldn't have gone off to Maine and left the necklace hidden in the Hall of Dinosaurs.

"Nancy . . ."

Nancy jumped as the voice spoke right behind her. She glanced around. Dan Stevens had come into the hall while she was talking to Ruthie, and now he was staring up at the turtle with an odd look on his face. Nancy looked at him uneasily. Had he too noticed that golden sparkle of light from the fossilized bones? But, no, Dan was smiling as his eyes swept from Archelon around to the other exhibits in the hall.

"These things bug me," he said with a shrug. Then, "There's a heck of a storm blowing up, Nancy. Better hustle out of here. Mr. Baron wants to close up."

Nancy stood up. "Will you call a taxi for me, Dan? Ruthie's mother will be worrying . . ."

"Sure thing." He hurried back to the entrance hall.

Nancy glanced uncertainly at the turtle. She longed to explore the little niche and get the necklace, if that was what it really was, but not with Ruthie watching. The fewer people who knew about this, the better.

"Let's go," she said to Ruthie.

By the time they reached the entrance hall, Dan had run upstairs to make sure that all visitors were out of the upper rooms. Mr. Baron was about to tour the lower rooms before putting out the lights.

"Get going right away, Nancy," he said. "This storm is going to be a humdinger." He moved away down the corridor to the Wildlife Hall—the corridor where, earlier, Nancy had fancied for a moment that she had seen Alan. Outside, a horn sounded. The taxi was waiting at the curb. The girls flew down the walk in the gloom of a murky sky, and Nancy pushed Ruthie into the cab.

"I must take care of Miss May's cat," she said. "Please call my mother as soon as you get home, Ruthie, and tell her that I'll wait the storm out at Miss May's. We'll have that soda some other day." She shut the door and the taxi drove off with Ruthie's face pressed against the window.

Nancy ran back to the museum through a spatter of raindrops as big as nickels. Thunder was growling in the sky. The thick, humid air was breathlessly still as nature waited for the storm to break.

Inside the museum, Nancy paused to consider what she should do next. Smilodon came padding out of the shop to join her. She picked the cat up in her arms. She couldn't go into the Hall of Dinosaurs now—she'd meet Mr. Baron on his way back to the entrance hall.

And Dan would be coming downstairs at any minute. She glanced about hurriedly. Then, still carrying Smilodon, she ran to the supply closet set in an angle of the hall. After Mr. Baron had passed the closet, she would slip out and dash into the Hall of Dinosaurs to get the necklace. When she returned to the entrance hall, Mr. Baron would think she had been chasing the cat.

"Now be still, Smilodon," she cautioned, closing the closet door to a tiny crack.

The cat did not like being shut up in the closet. He gave a plaintive meow and pawed at her leg.

"Shh!" Nancy whispered, stooping to pet him.

His claw caught in her stocking, starting a run. "Now see what you've done!" Nancy scolded.

Outside, there sounded the bang of the museum door being pulled shut. That must be Dan going out. Nancy peered through the crack in the door. Her eyes blinked as a glare of lightning lit the dimness outside. A booming roll of thunder followed. Nancy flinched. She didn't like thunderstorms one bit!

Suddenly it seemed to her that her plan for getting the topazes from Archelon's skeleton was childish and melodramatic. The sensible thing would be to find Mr. Baron and ask him to help her. She pushed the closet door open and stepped into the hall. The first thing that struck her was the utter stillness inside the museum. All the lights were out except for the night light near the door. Oh, great heavens! What if Mr. Baron had left the museum with Dan!

She looked helplessly up at the tall leaded windows

on either side of the massive door. Gusty winds were whipping through the rain-swept darkness outside. Nancy gave a low cry as lightning cut the gloom like a white-hot blade and a clap of thunder from directly overhead seemed to rock the building. She ran to the door and tried the knob. The door was locked! Mr. Baron had indeed gone home and she was alone in the museum—locked in for the night!

Nancy pressed her two hands to her mouth while panic churned inside her. The wind was driving sheets of rain across the portico and against the windows. There was no hope of escape through those windows— only a few of the small panes opened. The only other windows on the ground floor were in Professor Craig's office. She darted across the hall to the office door and tried it frantically. It was locked. She turned away in despair and then jumped nervously at another sharp flash and a roll of thunder.

Suddenly, in her mind's eye, she saw a little red light burning at the end of the Hall of Dinosaurs. She drew a quivery breath. Of course! She could get out through the fire door. She'd collect the necklace from Archelon on her way through the hall, then run across to Miss May's house to wait until the storm was over.

"Come along, Smilodon," she said to the cat.

A flash of lightning illumined the windows with a blue glare. Thunder roared and crackled ominously close. There was a resounding crash outside, and the light in the entrance hall went out. Smilodon gave a howl and tore into the shop to hide. Nancy stood frozen with terror. She held her breath, waiting for the next flash, then dared to breathe a little more easily when the next boom seemed to come from a greater distance.

In the dim light, Nancy made her way to one of the windows and peered out. Storm clouds still hung low and black over the city. Lightning flashed again. Rain was coming down in torrents. Nancy could see dimly that one of the big elms near the museum was down. Evidently it had dragged the power lines down with it. She wondered uneasily if Ruthie had reached home safely and if she had telephoned the Paynes to assure her mother that she was safe at Miss May's house.

11

Peril among the dinosaurs

The light inside the thick walls of the museum was like a murky twilight. There were thick shadows at the turn of the staircase and where the corridors stretched away. The stillness pressed in on Nancy. Then her heart jumped as she thought she heard something move on the stairs.

"Smilodon," she called softly. "Come on—let's get out of here." But Smilodon stayed hidden in the shop. Nancy shrugged and stopped calling. The cat would be safe enough if he preferred to spend the night in the museum rather than venture out into the wild night. She wasn't going to linger there coaxing him.

She started toward the doorway to the Hall of Dinosaurs, only to pause, like a deer poised for flight, as a whisper of sound reached her through the eerie silence. This time it came from the direction of the Hall of Wildlife. She thought she heard something bump and then a crystalline crash—or was it a crash of thunder? Nervously she peered along the dusky corridor, thinking of the dead bear, the moose, the lynx with their glassy eyes. Did they stir in their cases when the museum closed for the night and come back to life like the toys in an old fairy tale?

Nancy laughed shakily at her childish fancy. The next moment she gave a broken cry as a small body darted past her and made off into the shadows of the corridor.

"Oh! Smilodon!" Nancy gave a half-sob. The cat must have heard a rat stirring about down there. But the idea of a rat being on the premises did nothing to calm her jittery nerves. She walked quickly across the dusky hall to the doorway of the Hall of Dinosaurs. She wasn't going to waste any more time before she found the topazes and got out of this spooky building.

In the doorway, she paused, reluctant to venture in among the monster skeletons. Faintly seen through the gloom, they seemed to take on menacing life. She raised a shaky hand to brush back the damp hair from her forehead. Don't be silly, she told herself, they're nothing but a lot of old bones!

Archelon stood near the doorway, where the shadows were not quite so thick. Nancy's footsteps echoed loudly as she hurried over to the turtle. She stepped up on the cement block on which the giant skeleton was mounted, and standing on tiptoe with her arm raised high, she reached for the little niche in the vertebra where her eyes had caught the golden sparkle of a topaz. A grunt of exasperation came from her. She was about half an inch too short to reach the niche!

She drew a deep breath and prepared to try again. Suddenly the feeling that she was being watched came over her. A creepy sensation tightened the roots of her hair and her heart gave a frightened lurch. She glanced nervously over her shoulder, but only the stark skeletons of the dinosaurs were there to stare at her through the darkness with their empty eye sockets. She turned hastily back to the turtle and strained high on her toes to claw breathlessly at the recess with her fingertips. She missed it and tried again, jumping this time to give herself added height. Her fingers closed on something cold and hard—links of topaz and diamond!

"Eureka!" she murmured, her cheeks hot with triumph.

With the necklace clutched tightly in her fist, she jumped down, and then some instinctive warning of danger caused her to whirl around to face the doorway to the entrance hall. A bulky figure was rushing at her in deadly silence!

Terror swelled in Nancy's throat. She gave a choked scream and fled down the long hall to the fire door. Footsteps clattered behind her. She dodged around a block on which a prehistoric crocodile was mounted, its long jaws seeming to reach for her in the darkness. She stumbled over the corner of the block, righted herself, and ran on, sobbing in panic. Her pursuer gained, still in that dreadful silence. A hand grabbed her shoulder. Nancy squirmed sideways, toward the largest dinosaur, flailing out wildly with her arm and holding the necklace in her other hand.

"Help!" she screamed, even though there was no one to hear her but her faceless antagonist. "Help! Help! Help!"

This was no phantom prehistoric monster she was battling, but a strong and determined man. He seized her arm and twisted it cruelly as he tore the necklace from her fingers. In the dim light Nancy saw that he wore a workman's cap pulled low and that a handkerchief covered the lower part of his face. There was something vaguely familiar about his general appearance, but she had no time to ponder on what it was.

He had the necklace now and her fingers were tingling with pain where the jewels had scraped her skin when she had tried to keep hold of them. The man shoved her away hard and made for the fire door. In another moment, he would be gone into the rainy night with the topaz necklace. Breathing hard from the struggle, Nancy peered after him. She knew that her mother would always believe that it was Alan who had assaulted her and stolen the necklace.

No! She couldn't just stand there and let Alan be unjustly accused! She dashed after the thief and caught up with him near the fire door, where the corridor to the Hall of Wildlife led away into darkness. With a determined cry, she snatched at the handkerchief that covered his face. It came away in her hand, but at the same moment the man swung his arm and sent her reeling away from him. She fell heavily against the concrete block on which the stegosaurus was mounted. She gasped with pain, but struggled instantly to her feet, still holding the handkerchief-mask.

The thief was at the fire door now, fumbling with the bolt. Oddly, he was illumined by a beam of strong light. Had the power gone on again? Nancy wondered, still a little dazed with pain. Then she realized what it was —the beam of a flashlight flooding out of the Hall of Wildlife. With a start of wonderment she heard Alan's voice, and then she saw Alan himself bolt out of the corridor toward the man at the fire door. He grabbed him just as the door swung open.

During the desperate silent struggle that followed, Alan's flashlight fell to the floor. Nancy ran to pick it up and turn it on the two men. She gave a low cry as she recognized the thief. It was Dan Stevens!

Dan pulled himself away from Alan, and as Alan went for him again, he thrust out a foot and tripped him. Alan sprawled on the floor, and in a flash Dan plunged out of the door and was swallowed up in the tumult of wind and rain.

Alan picked himself up off the floor. "A lot of help I was," he said ruefully. Then in an anxious voice, he added, "Are you all right, Nancy? I heard you scream and came running."

Nancy rubbed her bruised arm. "I—I guess I'm all right." Her smile was a little tremulous. "But he got away with the topaz necklace."

"Who was it? Or don't you know?"

"It was Dan Stevens."

Crushed by a feeling of defeat, she sat down at the base of the stegosaurus. It was hard to believe that it was Dan who had mauled her so roughly and stolen the topazes. She wondered wearily if he had taken the necklace the night of the banquet, or if he had just happened to spot the hiding place of the jewels that afternoon and decided to help himself. And Alan? What was he doing in the museum after hours? Not that she wasn't thankful for his presence.

Alan was just as curious about her own presence in the museum after closing time.

"What's been going on?" he demanded. "How come you're here at this hour? How did you know that Stevens had the necklace?"

"Because he took it away from me."

Nancy told her story.

"Whew!" Alan pulled out his handkerchief and wiped his face. "There sure has been a lot going on in this old bone dump tonight."

The fire door still swung open. The electrical storm had passed and the new-washed breath of the windy night felt cool and refreshing as it swept into the Hall of Dinosaurs. Most of the storm clouds had blown away and the light was stronger now. Nancy switched off the flashlight. Then she started as something soft rubbed against her legs. It was only Smilodon. She stooped to stroke him.

"I wondered how Miss May came to leave him shut up in the museum," said Alan.

"I was supposed to take him home."

"He must have heard me or smelled me, because he came looking for me."

Now it was Nancy's turn to ask questions. "What were you doing in the Hall of Wildlife? Miss May said you were leaving for Maine right after work, but now

I know I wasn't just imagining things when I fancied I saw you in the corridor late this afternoon." She drew a deep breath. "I wish I had known you were in the building when the storm was worst. Was I ever scared!"

"Well, I certainly never dreamed there was anyone around but me. I hid in the little passageway on which the backs of the display cases open and waited until I felt sure that Mr. Baron had locked up and gone home." He looked down at her, his dark hair tousled from his struggle with Dan. "Nancy, there's something I've wanted to tell you for a long time. I'm going to take Big Black home with me and bury his pelt decently in the woods where he used to roam. That's what brought me to Glendale Falls—not any desire to take vengeance on your stepfather."

Nancy's lips parted. She stared at Alan in stunned amazement. "You'll never get away with such a crazy scheme!" she burst out.

Alan frowned. "Why not? I've already got Black through the door at the back of his case. I broke some glass in the process, but I'll send the museum money to pay for it."

"So that's the sound I heard! I thought the animals had come to life." Nancy began to laugh shakily; then she sobered as she realized fully what Alan had said.

"You can help me get Black out to my station wagon, as long as you're here," Alan continued. "I found a dolly in the passageway that they use for moving the mounted animals. The station wagon's parked around in back. We'll push Black up here and take him out through this door. That was my original plan, but it would have been a lot more difficult to carry out by myself."

"Alan! We can't steal the bear from the museum!" Nancy protested.

"We won't be stealing him because he doesn't belong here," Alan said firmly. "Oh, I know the law gave your stepfather a license to shoot a bear, but not a tame bear —not *my* bear!"

"We'd be arrested."

"After I get Black back to his own country, I don't care whether I'm arrested or not," Alan said with a reckless glint in his eyes. "And no one need ever know that you helped me."

"I would know."

Nancy stood up. She was on the verge of tears. She understood and sympathized with Alan's feelings about the bear, but she couldn't go along with this rash plan of his—and neither would she abandon him. She felt torn in two directions.

"You just can't do such a thing, Alan," she said, twisting her hands together nervously. "What would Cousin Burton think of you—and Miss May?"

"Not much, I'm afraid." There was a ring of regret in Alan's voice, but his jaw was set firmly. "Both of them suspect I've got plans of some sort, and they've tried to talk me into forgetting about my grudge over Big Black's murder."

"They're your friends and you couldn't do better than to listen to them." Nancy moved closer to Alan. She simply had to find the right words to move him!

"Big Black is dead, Alan. You won't do him or yourself any good by dragging him back to the woods, and you'd be taking him away from the kids who come to the museum. They love Black best of all the exhibits. If you saw how their eyes shine when they stand there, you wouldn't dream of taking him away. Most of the children will never see a wild bear, but from looking at Black they get some idea of what it means to be a bear free in the woods. If you take him away, you'll be robbing all the girls and boys who come to the museum of a thrilling experience in natural history."

Alan's face had softened a little while she was speaking. "You're a pretty good persuader," he said with a note of tenderness in his voice.

"I'm only telling you the truth. And another thing, it will be a wicked shame, Alan Shelby, if you throw away your chance of going to college, not to mention helping Cousin Burton with his important work, in order to haul a bearskin up to the mountains! You'd do better to concentrate on a useful career in conservation. Then you could feel that you were really doing something to preserve bears and other species that are being destroyed by mankind. It would be a fitting monument to Big Black," she added softly. "Something that would really count."

She slipped her hand through Alan's arm. "I won't help you make off with Big Black, but I'll help you put him back in his case, and I'll go with you to Cousin Burton while you explain what happened. I'll even help you pay for that broken glass."

"What a pal you are, Nancy!" he exclaimed bitterly. "You'll do everything but what I ask you to do. And I suppose, if I try to get Black out by myself, you'll go yelling for the police . . ."

Nancy pulled her arm away, deeply hurt by his words. "You know I'd do nothing of the sort."

"I'm sorry, Nancy," Alan said quickly. "I didn't mean that—honest."

"It's all right," she murmured.

"A fellow can't give up in a moment what he's been planning for a year," Alan muttered. After a moment of inward struggle, he admitted, "I guess I've been pretty childish about this plan to take Black back home."

"Let's get him back in his case," Nancy said eagerly.

But just then voices sounded outside. Alan and Nancy turned to look out through the fire door. Three people were walking across the drenched grass from Miss May's house. Through the early dusk, flashlights played on the museum. Burton Payne's voice said, "That fire door is open."

A big man in a raincoat strode ahead of the others. "Nancy!" he shouted as he neared the door. "Nancy, are you in there?"

Nancy had been so wrapped up in Alan's problems that she had forgotten the earlier events of the afternoon—and even the topaz necklace. Now the sound of her stepfather's voice brought it all back. Suddenly she felt utterly exhausted.

"I'm here, Mr. Payne," she answered in a small voice.

12

Who stole the Payne topazes?

Mr. Payne stepped through the fire door and flashed his powerful torchlight around the shadowy hall. He gave a sharp exclamation when he recognized Alan; then he put his arm protectively around Nancy's shoulders.

"What a scare you gave me, young lady," he scolded. "Ruthie Webster telephoned your mother that you were going to stay with Miss May until the storm was over. When the worst had passed, I drove here to take you home—only to discover that you hadn't been near the house. Then Burton came in with word that the big elm in front of the museum had been struck by lightning." His arm tightened about her, and his voice grew husky with emotion. "I was afraid that you'd been hit by that falling tree and were lying out there in the rain."

"I'm sorry to have been such a worry to you," Nancy said. She felt strangely secure inside the circle of her stepfather's strong arm.

Miss May and Burton Payne had followed Oliver into the museum.

"So you were here all the time, safe and dry," Miss May said to Nancy with relief in her voice. "And Smilodon too, thank goodness. I was anxious when he didn't come home." She lifted the purring cat in her arms and gave Alan an inquiring glance over his furry head. "How do you happen to be here, Alan? I thought you were on your way to Maine."

Her words caused Oliver Payne to give Alan a sharp glance.

"I had some work to do before going home." Alan's eyes met Nancy's in a look of conspiracy. "It's all finished now."

"Where is Mr. Baron?" Miss May asked, glancing around.

"He went home early today," Nancy answered. "And accidentally left me locked inside the museum."

"Well, that was a careless piece of bungling, I must say!" boomed Oliver Payne.

Nancy was quick to defend the old caretaker. "It wasn't Mr. Baron's fault. I was hiding in the closet . . ."

Miss May and the two men stared at her. After a moment Oliver Payne sighed deeply, as if he wondered if he would ever get to understand this stepdaughter of his. "Just why were you hiding in the closet?" he asked, making an obvious effort to be patient.

"Well, you see, this afternoon I discovered that the topaz necklace was hidden in the skeleton of Archelon, the prehistoric turtle."

If she had dropped a bomb on her listeners, they

could scarcely have looked more startled. Her stepfather let his arm drop and stared at her, stunned. Burton Payne uttered a sharp exclamation, and Miss May's lips formed an amazed "Ohh!"

Oliver Payne found his voice. "Why didn't you telephone me?"

"I wanted to be smart, I guess, and surprise Mother and you by coming home with a pocketful of topazes and diamonds. I *would* have telephoned when I realized that I was locked in, but then there was that awful thunderbolt that struck the tree and knocked out the power."

"Oh, Nancy," Miss May murmured. "How terribly frightened you must have been."

"I was scared almost out of my wits," Nancy admitted. "But then I remembered the fire door. I meant to get the necklace and go out that way, and over to your house, but—there was someone else in the museum."

"You mean this boy?" her stepfather demanded.

"No. Not Alan. I had just got the necklace down from the turtle skeleton . . ."

"Where is it?" Oliver Payne demanded. He held out his hand. "Give it to me!"

"I—I haven't got it."

"What? But you said . . ."

"Why don't you let Nancy finish her story?" Miss May put in.

"Nancy, where's the necklace?" Mr. Payne shouted so violently that Nancy took a step back from him.

"I'm trying to tell you, if you'll only let me!" she an-

swered, tense and tightlipped. What if Mr. Payne completely lost his temper when he learned that his precious necklace had disappeared again! She glanced at
Miss May and received an encouraging pat on her arm.
Nancy drew a deep breath. "A masked man rushed at
me and grabbed the necklace."

"A masked man? What kind of a fantasy are you trying to put over on us?" Mr. Payne turned his head and
scowled at Alan. "Nancy, I think you're trying to shield
someone."

"I am not! I tell you a masked man was hiding near
the doorway and he took the necklace away from me."
Nancy blinked to hold back a storm of tears. She felt
so unutterably tired. She longed to bolt through the
fire door and run away to some place where she
wouldn't be shouted at or grilled with questions.

"Oliver, don't upset the child," Miss May said. "Can't
you see that she's been through a terrible experience?"

Mr. Payne gave Miss May an impatient glance, but
when he turned back to Nancy, his manner was not
quite so domineering.

"I don't mean to be rough on you, Nancy, but remember, that necklace is extremely valuable. Now—
have you any clue to the identity of the masked man?"

"It was Dan Stevens."

"Dan Stevens!" Miss May exclaimed, incredulous.

"I pulled his mask off while we were struggling . . ."
Miss May was horrified, and so were the two men.

"He knocked me down when I tried to get the necklace back." Nancy clenched her hands as she relived

that sickening moment. "Then Alan heard me scream, and he and Dan fought."

Alan's mouth quirked in a grin that had no humor in it. "And a lot of help I was."

"Dan got away through the fire door," Nancy finished. "And took the topazes with him."

Oliver Payne exploded. "I'll settle with that fellow when I catch up with him."

"Nancy, dear," said Miss May. "If I had gone through such an ordeal, I'd be in screaming hysterics. You're a brave girl. But how could we have been so wrong about Dan?" She clicked her tongue. "A thief and a bully!"

"I wonder if it really was Dan who took the necklace in the first place," Nancy said thoughtfully. "If he had, wouldn't he have recovered it from the skeleton before today?"

"That's good reasoning, Nancy," said Cousin Burton. "If Dan had stolen the necklace to sell it, he wouldn't have risked leaving it here for so long."

"I had the feeling that Dan discovered the hiding place at the same time I did—this afternoon," Nancy continued. "He was standing right behind me. He's been desperate about where to find the money for a new car," she remembered.

Miss May nodded. "Lucille," she murmured—a remark understood only by Nancy and herself. "Well, no matter who took the necklace in the first place, you know where to look for it now, Oliver."

Oliver Payne frowned from under his heavy brows. "It's important to know who the original thief was, too.

Nancy, I believe that you failed to get in touch with me immediately, when you discovered the necklace, because you suspected who had hidden it and were trying to shield him."

Burton Payne made an exasperated sound.

"No!" said Nancy. Tiredly she raised her hand to push back her hair.

"Were you trying to shield Alan Shelby?" Mr. Payne persisted.

"No, no!" Nancy cried.

Burton Payne's voice cracked like a whip. "Watch what you're saying, Oliver! Alan is no thief."

"I'm not so sure. I've put up with his brash threats and suspicious actions because Nancy liked him and refused to believe anything bad about him—but this time he's gone too far." He shook his finger at Alan. "You've not explained your presence in this building after hours! You were here to get that necklace you had stolen, weren't you? You planned to start for Maine tonight and take the topazes with you."

"I don't know anything about your miserable necklace—and care less," Alan replied hotly.

"You stole that necklace in order to get even with me for shooting Big Black!" thundered Mr. Payne.

"I did not! I'm no more a thief than you are." Alan clenched his fists, looking as if he would like to punch Mr. Payne in the nose. Burton stepped between them.

"Oliver, you're talking like an idiot," Burton said calmly. "No one stole the topazes. They were taken by their rightful owner—me."

"What's that you say?" Oliver seemed unable to believe his ears.

Miss May, Nancy, and Alan all stared at Burton, speechlessly. He smiled at them, his eyes bright behind his dark-rimmed glasses.

"I picked the necklace off the floor the night of the banquet, when you and John and I came back to search the hall. When I saw the topazes glittering there, under a bench where someone must have kicked them, I felt that a just fate had delivered my property into my hands. I hid the necklace in the turtle skeleton because that was the handiest place—the rest of you were searching the corridor to the Hall of Wildlife."

"Burton!" Miss May cried out, scandalized.

"You needn't be upset, Annie," Burton told her. "The topazes really belong to me—Grandmother meant for me to have them. Their value means nothing to me— the important thing was getting them out of Oliver's greedy hands. So I hid them in Archelon's ancient bones, intending to leave them there, a mystery forever unsolved. But I didn't reckon with a young girl's bright eyes," he added with a whimsical smile.

"By Jove," shouted Oliver Payne, "I ought to have you arrested! I wouldn't have expected even you to pull off such a sneaky trick." He was almost bursting with rage, and he looked so ugly that Nancy made a mental vow never to permit herself to lose her temper again.

Burton Payne remained as cool as Oliver was tempestuous. It was plain that he enjoyed having riled his cousin's quick temper.

"Perhaps you *should* call the police and denounce me as a thief," he said calmly. "You'd have to go into court and swear that Grandmother never told you in my presence that I was to have the Payne topazes. Are you prepared to do that, Cousin Oliver?"

Oliver chewed his lower lip and glared at Burton from under his heavy brows. Burton, for his part, wore a mocking little smile on his thin, intellectual face.

"Come, come, Oliver. Aren't you going to call the police?"

Oliver reminded Nancy of a big bear brought to bay. "You know full well that I'll do nothing of the kind," he rumbled.

"Ah! Then you admit that I was within my rights in hiding the necklace?"

"Never!" was the indignant answer. Then Oliver Payne amazed everyone by adopting a conciliatory tone. "I'm the oldest, and the topazes belong in my branch of the family. That's surely the way Grandmother would have wanted it, if she had been able to think things out clearly during the last days of her life."

"It's easy for you with that sort of twaddle to justify yourself," Burton sneered.

"Gentlemen," Miss May spoke up impatiently. "Perhaps I had better remind you that at present neither one of you is in possession of the Payne topazes and that if you ever want to see them again, you'd better get in touch with the police so they can apprehend Dan Stevens."

Burton stared at her and then gave a snort of laughter. "You're right, my dear. While Oliver and I stand here quarreling like a couple of schoolboys, that rascal Stevens is making off with the loot."

"Let's go over to my house," Miss May suggested. "The telephone may be working again by now."

Oliver Payne nodded. "I must call my wife and let her know what's delayed us."

He insisted that Nancy put on his raincoat. Then, in his authoritive manner, he herded all the others ahead of him out of the museum and closed the fire door carefully. Outside, he touched his cousin's arm. Burton glanced at him inquiringly. Oliver cleared his throat— then he said urgently, "When we tell the police about the theft of the topazes from the museum, I suggest that we leave the identity of the person who placed the necklace in the skeleton a mystery—and a secret among this little group. The controversy over the ownership of the necklace is something that concerns only you and me, Burton. Shall we leave it that way?"

"That suits me," Burton said. He swept a humorous glance over the little group standing in the shadow of the museum. The rain had slackened to a gentle mist, and their faces glistened with moisture as they looked back at him. "What do you say, gang? Will you all conspire to keep me out of the jailhouse?"

Nancy giggled. Alan came out with a solemn, "Yes, sir, if you'll do the same for me."

Burton shot him an inquiring look, but just then Miss May broke in. "It will have to be made clear to the police that Nancy is certain Dan was not the original thief. It could have an influence on his case."

"Yes," Oliver agreed. He turned to Burton. "You

think the topazes are rightfully yours. And I feel just as strongly that they belong to me. But shall we shake hands, Burt? We used to be pretty good friends when we were boys."

Burton dropped his jaunty manner and held out his hand. Oliver grasped it strongly. Then, as if each felt slightly embarrassed over this show of emotion, they started across the wet grass toward Miss May's house, Burton with his hand under Miss May's elbow.

"I'm glad the feud is over—they've been acting like a couple of mean little kids," Nancy whispered to Alan as they walked behind the others.

"I'll say," he agreed. "And people have the nerve to talk about the delinquent younger generation!"

Up ahead, Miss May was saying, "There's been so much hard feeling over those topazes, it might be a good thing for the Payne family if they were never heard of again."

Both Burton and Oliver were quick to disagree with her. They might battle about who had the best claim to the necklace, but it had to stay in the family. Dan Stevens must be caught and punished, and the topazes must be returned to their real owner.

"And which one is that?" Nancy murmured to Alan. She chuckled. "I'm sure my stepfather and Cousin Burton would feel as if they were missing some of the spice of life if they didn't have those topazes to quarrel over. Why, they've completely forgotten that they never did find out what you were doing in the museum, Alan." She knew that Miss May had not forgotten, but that wise woman was keeping her own counsel.

The three older people passed through Miss May's gate with Smilodon trotting ahead, eager for his long-delayed supper. Alan paused and reached for Nancy's hand to keep her from following the others.

"I want you to know that I'm going to leave Black in the museum," he said in a low voice.

She drew a deep breath of happiness. "Oh, Alan, I'm so glad! That beautiful display will be *your* gift to all the children who come to the museum, even though Oliver Payne's name will be on the case."

"And I'll have Black, too, in memory—the way he was when he roamed free in the woods." He squeezed her hand affectionately. "Thanks, Nancy, for helping me see it that way."

The power company's crew had only just arrived to chop away the tangle of tree limbs from in front of the museum, and it would be several hours before the lights and telephones in that part of the city could be restored. Mr. Payne and Nancy left for home at once, and Mr. Payne stopped at the police station on the way to report the theft of the topazes. He looked very grave when he returned to the car.

"Young Stevens' car skidded on the wet pavement while he was driving away from the museum and hit another car," he said, as he got behind the wheel.

Nancy shuddered. She could imagine only too well at what a killing speed Dan had been driving.

"Both cars are total wrecks," Mr. Payne continued. "The drivers are in the hospital. Dan is in a serious condition, and the police won't be able to question him tonight. But the hospital attendants found the necklace in his coat pocket and put it away in the hospital safe. I'll claim it in the morning."

Nancy was staring soberly through the windshield at the road ahead, remembering how once she had ripped along it with Dan in his little red car. People like Dan shouldn't be allowed to drive, she reflected. They had no sense of responsibility toward other drivers, and sooner or later they crashed, and then innocent people were hurt.

She herself felt no rancor toward Dan, in spite of his rough handling of her in the museum. She hadn't been a person to Dan. For him, only Lucille and he really existed in this world, but now he would be all alone, for certainly Lucille was not the type to stand by a friend who had got himself into such a mess.

Nancy hoped, if Dan recovered from his injuries, that she would never have to appear in court to testify against him in the case of the Payne topazes.

As it turned out, Dan made a full confession the next day when Mr. Payne was allowed to visit him with a city detective.

Miss May and Burton Payne had driven over to the Payne house and, with Mrs. Payne and the two girls, were waiting in the living room to hear Oliver's story when he returned from the hospital. He told them that Dan had also confessed to stealing the peridots that had disappeared from the mineral room at the museum earlier that summer. He had intended to have them set into some jewelry for his girl, but had always lacked the cash to carry out his plan.

"It seemed to relieve his mind to confess all this," Mr. Payne continued. "And to know the jewels would be returned to their owners. Evidently he didn't plan either of the robberies—someone else really did break the glass in the museum gem case, maybe by leaning on it—and Dan saw his opportunity and grabbed the gems. That young man has to sort things out in his mind and recognize his responsibility toward his fellow men and their property. By the way, Nancy, he sent you a message: He hopes he didn't hurt you in the struggle for the topazes, but you should have known better than to get in his way!"

"*Well!*" Mrs. Payne exclaimed angrily. "He really is incorrigible."

"Did you get the topazes, Father?" Karen asked suddenly.

Her father gave his booming laugh. "I'd almost forgotten them!" He pulled the necklace from his pocket and placed it on a table, where it lay in dazzling splendor. Karen cried out in pleasure, but Mrs. Payne looked at the jewels with deep aversion.

"I'll never wear the necklace again, Oliver," she said. "I'd always be thinking of all the trouble it's caused."

"Annie feels the same way about the necklace," Burton Payne put in. "She tells me that when she becomes my wife she'd as soon be caught wearing the toe bones of my stegosaurus for jewels as the Payne topazes."

Nancy chuckled delightedly. Karen stared at Miss May and then at her stepmother, as though she couldn't understand their attitude toward such beautiful jewels.

"So, Oliver," Burton continued, "I propose that, since neither your wife nor my wife-to-be will wear our necklace, we put the topazes in trust for Karen until she comes of age."

Karen let out a squeal of delight. "You mean Great-grandmother's necklace is to be mine? Oh, fabulous! I can't wait to wear it."

"You won't be wearing it for a number of years," her father reminded her. He turned to his cousin. "That's a generous gesture, Burt." The two men exchanged friendly grins.

"Which one of us do you suppose Grandmother really meant to have the topazes?" Oliver wondered.

"Why, me, of course," was Burton's prompt reply.

Oliver scowled at his cousin, then he burst into a hearty laugh. The two women and the girls chimed in happily, relieved to know that the long feud over the Payne topazes was over.

Minnie Bell came to the living room door. "There's a young man out here who wants to see Mrs. Payne."

With a suspicion of whom the caller might be, Nancy followed her mother into the hall. Alan was standing by the outside door, as if he were not sure of a welcome. Mrs. Payne stopped when she saw him. Nancy hovered worriedly in the background.

"You asked for me?" Nancy's mother said coldly.

"Yes'm." Alan was neatly dressed in clean jeans and a sport shirt. His dark hair was slicked back and his ruddy-dark skin had a healthy glow. "I'm off for Maine, but I'll be coming back in the fall to live with Burton Payne and go to high school in Glendale Falls."

Mrs. Payne looked anything but happy over this bit of information, but Nancy's face broke into a delighted smile. Alan must have cleared up the matter of Big Black, and now there was nothing to stand between him and the bright promise of his future!

"Why have you come to tell me this?" Mrs. Payne asked. She turned her head to give Nancy an irritated look, as if to say that she understood the reason very well.

Alan shifted his feet uncomfortably. "I guess I didn't make a very good impression on you the last time I was here."

"That's putting it mildly." Mrs. Payne's eyes looked hard as sapphires. "To be frank, Alan, I would prefer that Nancy not associate with you."

Nancy gasped. "Mother!"

Surely Alan would go away now and she'd never see him again—the only boy she had ever wanted for a friend! But to her surprise, Alan stood his ground.

"Nancy can't help associating with me, since we'll be going to the same school," he pointed out. "But I want our friendship to be out in the open. That's why I came here today—to say good-by to Nancy openly. And to ask your permission to come here to see her when I return in the fall."

Nancy's eyes shone. Alan was like a breath of bracing pine scented air after Dan Stevens' devious ways. Oh, how could her mother help but like him?

Mrs. Payne had indeed lost a little of her hostile manner, but her eyes were still not friendly. "You can hardly expect me to welcome you while you're nursing that bitter grudge against Nancy's father," she told him.

Alan took an eager step toward her. "If I still had that grudge against Mr. Payne, I wouldn't have come near his house. But I've no time nor wish to hate him any more. I have more important things to do."

"Hello, Alan," said a hearty voice. Mr. Payne had stepped into the hall.

His wife turned to him with a perplexed expression. "This boy has come to see Nancy, and he says he no longer hates you for shooting that bear."

"I'm happy to hear that, my boy." Mr. Payne held out his hand.

To Nancy's consternation, Alan apparently did not see the outstretched hand. He was frowning at her stepfather.

"It's true that I've grown up a little this summer, and I'm no longer juvenile enough to hate you, Mr. Payne. But I hate the thing you did in shooting Black!" he said passionately. "I told Mrs. Payne that I have better things to do than to nourish a grudge—and I have! I'm going to get an education, with the help of your cousin. I'm going to work for conservation and try to educate other people to be conservation-minded." His clear gray eyes met Mr. Payne's accusingly. "And then someday maybe there will be fewer gun-happy, so-called sportsmen blazing away in the woods in the belief that killing off our vanishing wildlife somehow makes them big heroic fellows."

Mrs. Payne's face had flushed during this speech. Mr. Payne stood frozen, his eyes scowling from under his lowered brows. Nancy clenched her hands together. This would finish Alan with her family! Oh, why did he have to be so forthright!

The charged stillness in the hall was broken by Mr. Payne clearing his throat. "Maybe I deserved that lecture, Alan," he said heavily.

He turned to his wife. "This boy doesn't like me, but after all I'm not the one he wants to come here to see. If Nancy wants him to come, I feel that we should welcome him, too."

Mrs. Payne gave Alan an exasperated glance. Then she looked at Nancy, bright-eyed, anxious, and on her toes with eagerness as she waited for her mother's answer. Finally, with a deep sigh, she gave in.

"Very well," she said to Alan. "You may come here to see Nancy."

Nancy wished the invitation could have been more cordial, but the important thing was that it had been given.

Her mother went a step further. "Have a good trip to Maine, Alan."

With a stately but gracious nod, she went back into the living room. Mr. Payne lingered. There was an almost boyishly wistful expression on his handsome heavy face. Gratitude toward him welled up in Nancy.

"Thanks, Father, for persuading Mother," she said softly.

The word came out easily. Mr. Payne would never take the place of her own daddy, but Nancy felt humbled by the sudden realization of how this autocratic man had worked at being understanding, tolerant, and fatherly, ever since she had come to his house. Calling him "Father" was little enough to do in return. She was too independent and he was too dictatorial for their relations ever to be the same as those between him and Karen, but Nancy was surprised to discover how much she had come to like and respect her stepfather. He was a big man in every way, in his person, in his faults, but also in his virtues.

Mr. Payne beamed at her, then he turned to Alan.

"Your honesty demands a return in kind from me," he said earnestly. "I want you to know that I'm not proud of the way I shot Big Black. But at the time, I didn't really understand that he was a partly tame bear or that he meant so very much to you."

Alan's mouth quirked. Please don't say anything caustic, Alan! Nancy begged with her eyes.

"What you might like to know," Mr. Payne continued, "is that now that the Hall of Wildlife at the museum is complete, I intend to do all my future shooting with a camera." His eyes sparkled as the possibilities of this new hobby occurred to him. "I intend to start on a series of wildlife films to be presented to the museum."

A picture of the people at the midsummer banquets being entertained for years to come by Oliver Payne's wildlife films flashed through Nancy's mind. She could not contain a low chuckle, but she said with deep sincerity, "The children who come to the museum would love them." Her eyes implored Alan.

"They sure would," Alan chimed in stiffly. "It—it's a great project, Mr. Payne." The words came hard, but at least he had said them, and Mr. Payne looked pleased.

"Safe driving to Maine and back, young fellow," he said.

"Thank you, sir."

They did not offer to shake hands, but Nancy sensed that some of the tension between them had ebbed away.

"Walk to my car with me, Nancy," Alan invited.

He held the door open for her, and they crossed the porch and went down the steps together. Walking along the drive to where Alan's station wagon was parked, they held hands.

"Last night I told Uncle Burt—that's what I'm to call him now—about what I had done at the museum," Alan said. "He gave me a lecture on being juvenile, some of which I just passed on to your folks. But also, he went over there with me this morning and helped me put Black back in his case. He has a man there now, replacing the glass I broke, and the whole thing is to stay a secret known only to four people—you and me, Uncle Burt and Aunt Annie.

"I'm going to work at the lumber mill in my home town until school opens," he continued. "The pay is better than on the college maintenance force. It will pay for the glass I broke and give me money for school clothes—and for taking my girl out sometimes next winter." He gave Nancy his slow, contagious grin. "I don't want to depend on Uncle Burt for everything— he's being generous enough as it is."

Nancy nodded. "I know what you mean."

Suddenly Nancy felt that the sky had never been so blue before—that the sun had never shone so brightly. What a beautiful, wonderful world it was!

The smile that spilled out of her green eyes lent beauty to her face—but Alan had found that beauty long ago.